From Strays to Soulmates

KC McCormick Çiftçi

One

"Cheddar, get down from there!" Jasmine Brody marched across the floor, and the offending beast released its grip on the curtains of Kedi Cafe and dropped to the ground, scurrying underneath one of the far tables.

Jasmine surveyed the damage to the curtains, shaking her head as she tutted under her breath. It wasn't as if the airy white curtains were family heirlooms—she had picked them up at the bazaar just a few weeks ago, in fact—but the cafe itself was heirloom enough that anything that marred its perfectly imperfect facade was an offense.

She set off in search of Cheddar again. The orange demon was one of the newest additions to the fleet of cats awaiting customers every day at Kedi Cafe, a kitten from the nearby cat colony Jasmine was in the habit of feeding. He had followed her back to the cafe a few days ago, and he hadn't left. And even if he occasionally seemed to be possessed by a spirit that made him puff up his back, zoom across the floor, and climb her curtains, she had a soft spot for him.

"There you are, Cheddar." She crouched beside the table, and the young cat walked right out to her as if he had forgotten he had even had a reason to hide in the first place. He started purring immediately as he pranced his cocky kitten walk in circles around Jasmine, brushing up against her back and her shins in turn as she remained crouched in place.

"What are we going to do with you?" she asked. "I can't leave you here or you're going to destroy the place." She took in her grandmother's beloved cat cafe. Most restaurants in Istanbul had given up the fight to keep the city's many friendly strays from coming inside, often feeding them from the kitchen or letting them sleep on vacated chairs.

Kedi Cafe, though, took things a step farther, catering to the tourists who frequented the city. While there were cats to be seen and appreciated everywhere in the city, some tourists felt more comfortable with the idea of an "inside" cat than a friendly stray, even if the cats outside were likely every bit as clean and safe as most of the indoor ones. Jasmine had a great working relationship with Enes, a local veterinarian, who regularly received her business these days as she showed up with a new animal in need of immunizations and neutering on at least a weekly basis. He'd even given her a discount thanks to her repeat business.

There were three cats who lived full time in the cafe, as well as a courtyard behind the building that was equipped for ideal human-feline cohabitation. Cheddar, though...well, it seemed unlikely he would be joining the full-time crew at the cafe.

Which could only mean...

"You're coming home with me, sir. Where I can keep an eye on you and where there are no curtains for you to destroy. Yes, that's right," she cooed the last words at his pointed face, his whiskers vibrating as his purrs increased in volume. "And then you're coming back here again with me tomorrow, so you'd better get used to riding around in the cat backpack."

Cheddar followed Jasmine as she made her way back to the kitchen, where she began to gather the leftovers and cat food that she would take to the colony on her walk home. He meowed in protest and she dropped a few pieces of unseasoned chicken on the floor, as if by accident. She didn't need him thinking she was actually *responding* to his insistence. It was just a lucky coincidence, as far as he needed to know.

"Once you come live at my house, bud, you're going to have to learn not to beg." She shrugged to herself then, as if in acquiescence. "Not that Gator has stopped sniffing the air and meowing every time I open a can of tuna. And if you're still coming in to work with me here, then I guess you'll be singing for your supper every now and again."

Jasmine retrieved the cat backpack with its large plastic window that made it seem like the cat riding on her back was a visitor from outer space and placed it on the ground in front of Cheddar. As she crouched next to it to coax him inside, he bolted in before she could even get all the way to the ground. She looked at him in confusion and he blinked back up at her.

"Okay, then. That was easy." She placed a few more snacks inside—positive connotation was the key to success with a new experience like riding in the cat backpack—and lifted the carrier up. Cheddar seemed completely unbothered by his change in elevation and had, in fact, barely noticed it. Jasmine slipped the backpack on her shoulders, picked up the food for the cat colony, and made her way out the back door, locking it behind her.

When they were outside, she heard the first faint protest from Cheddar. "It's okay, bud," she offered over her shoulder. "We're going to visit your old home, and then you're coming to your new home."

With every step, she felt better about her decision to bring Cheddar to her apartment. The older cats who lived at the cafe full-time were well-behaved, subdued to the point where she had to encourage them to get a little bit of exercise with toys and treats that worked with diminishing effectiveness. Left to their own devices, they would move only to track the path of a sunbeam, and who was she to begrudge them that? Cabbage and Corduroy had come to Jasmine's grandmother years before, wandering to the door of the cafe a few months apart. Cabbage had arrived with a limp and Corduroy had been in need of a good bath and a flea treatment, and they had both never set foot outside again after their arrival day. The jury was still out on whether Grandma had domesticated them or if it had been the other way around, but they had been living a good life together ever since.

The thought of her grandmother brought an unexpected swell of emotion to Jasmine's throat. It had been over a month since she had seen her, since she had landed on Grandma's doorstep to run things in her absence while she took off on a world cruise with her boyfriend, Morty.

Grandma had never done anything like it before, and Jasmine was equal parts happy for her and worried about her.

Viola, Jasmine's grandmother, was from England, but she had spent her retirement in Turkey. Jasmine had fond memories of her first visit to Istanbul, and of the change she had seen in her grandmother during that first visit, her first winter away from England.

It had been a brighter time than the two of them were accustomed to, that was for sure. In Jasmine's childhood, she had looked forward to the plane ride to London after Christmas, a part of her family traditions that she could count on like clockwork. After celebrating the holiday with her mother's parents in Detroit, there would be an early morning journey to the airport, so early that it felt like the middle of the night, and then Viola, her father's mother, would meet them at Heathrow.

It always felt like the true beginning of winter, that visit. Though there was still the anticipation of New Year's Eve, the Christmas festivities had settled down and the cold had moved in. Viola's flat was chillier than Jasmine's home, and they all wore scarves and slippers in the house and drank more tea in a day than she normally drank in a month.

The days were short, too, of course, even though her dad liked to remind her that since it was after the winter solstice, every day was a little longer than the one before. Between the darkness and the cold, a wet cold that reached all the way to her bones, that trip brought with it a melancholy that Jasmine wouldn't be able to name or even identify until she was much older.

The first time she identified it was when she noted its absence, that first December day that she arrived in Istanbul to meet her grandmother in her new home.

It wasn't that it wasn't cold that day—no, there had been snow on the ground, though not as much as there had been back home in Grand Rapids. Perhaps it was that Christmas wasn't as widely celebrated, leaving the anticipation of the impending new year a very present focus.

The real change had been in Viola, though. There had been a lightness in her step as she showed Jasmine around her new neighborhood, stopping every so often to introduce her to yet another friendly street cat, all of which she had named.

"This is Pete. And that's Kahlua over there."

Jasmine had smiled at the names, at the lack of any rhyme or reason to them. There wasn't a theme, that much was clear. They seemed to come to her grandmother in a stream-of-consciousness fashion, and when Jasmine asked her why she had given a cat the name Pete, she had simply shrugged.

"That's just his name," she had said. "Why is your name Jasmine?"

"Because it's a nice name and Mom liked it, I guess. Well, you can't argue with logic like that," Jasmine had responded with a roll of her eyes.

Cabbage and Corduroy were two of those original cats, and Jasmine smiled at the thought of them, at the connection they provided between her and her grandmother even when Grandma was on the other side of the world.

The vacant lot where most of Viola's favorite felines lived was in sight now, the same place where Cheddar had lived just a few days ago, and Jasmine felt her lips stretch in a smile at the meow of recognition that reached her ears from just over her shoulder.

"That's right, bud. We're almost there. Smells familiar, huh?"

Cheddar made another sound, and Jasmine wondered what sort of response the cat colony elicited from him. Was he happy to be back? Traumatized by some memory of his life there? Or was he simply letting her know that he had had *more* than enough backpack time, thank you very much, and was ready to be set free to take out his feelings on another set of curtains?

Jasmine distributed the food she had brought, narrowly managing to do so without stepping on any tails as the herd of cats swarmed around her ankles, meowing with delight at the bounty she had brought. She cooed at them, greeting the familiar faces she saw and making a mental note of a few new arrivals. She would need to take one or two of them to see Enes if they stuck around, by the looks of it. In the far corner, closest to the wall of the building, she spotted a couple of small piles of kibble. She'd never seen them before, never seen any indication that anyone else was caring for this particular group of cats.

It stirred up the faintest twinge of an uncomfortable feeling, something she couldn't quite name. She noted a vague discomfort at the idea of someone else taking care of *her* cats, which was ridiculous given that there were more than enough cats here to go around. It was also ridiculous considering that the kibble was being ignored in favor of the leftovers she had brought from the cafe, which warmed

Jasmine with more pride than she would ever be willing to admit.

It was a short walk from the colony back to the apartment Viola had left in her care as well. Jasmine shook her head as she unlocked the door, Cheddar once again picking up the volume of his meows. How could it be that adjusted to her new life this quickly? That she felt so settled here with a business to run, a home to relax in, and even a few animal friends to care for, when just a few months ago she had been living paycheck to paycheck, putting up with roommates who had vastly different senses of hygiene than she did, simply because rent in Grand Rapids was too expensive for her artist's salary?

Well, salary *is the wrong word,* she thought. *You don't exactly get a regular salary when you're just picking up contracts that last for a short time.* And the fact was, that far more often than she got a commission to paint a beautiful mural on the side of a building, she was getting commissions to cover the side of the building with a single color of paint. It was the kind of job that college students took during the summer, and yet she accepted every one of those commissions that came her way. At least she was working with paint, in the end, even if it wasn't in the way in which she desired.

Thanks to the opportunity that Viola had given her, Jasmine wasn't taking any commissions these days. Or at least, she wasn't obligated to. She told herself that's why she hadn't so much as picked up a brush or dabbled on one of the blank canvases she had found locked away in the storage room at the cafe—Viola liked to paint, too. She had, in fact, been the first person to encourage Jasmine to explore her art. After one too many smiles-that-looked-more-like-grimaces from art teachers surveying her childhood creations, Jasmine had decided with an outsized level of authority that she was "not creative," and had immersed herself fully in the more left-brained subjects and activities her school had to offer.

It had been during one of her visits to her grandmother, one particularly wet and cold winter when the two of them had barely wanted to venture farther from the fireplace than to the kitchen to put on the kettle, that her grandmother had emerged from the spare bedroom's closet with brushes of all sizes and more colorful tubes of acrylic paint than Jasmine had seen outside of an arts and crafts supply store.

"What do you want me to do with that?" she had asked her grandmother, warily, noting the absence of any paper or canvas to paint on.

Viola had gestured towards the blank wall behind her. "Paint that," she had said. "I'm sick of looking at it. Make it interesting."

And that was all the instruction she had given. Jasmine had nearly come unraveled at the lack of guidance, the lack of expectations to meet. But after she had scrounged around for some old paper bags and newspapers to practice painting on, and after Viola had given a few approving clucks at the abstract swirls of color Jasmine had made there, she had gotten to work.

The resulting mural had been her grandmother's pride and joy, which had thrilled and embarrassed Jasmine in equal parts. The paint was barely dry before her grandmother had invited all of her friends over for a dinner party, during which she had insisted they go around the table sharing their favorite things about the mural.

But Viola had been onto something, as Jasmine had only realized years later. Her excessive praise and celebration of the abstract mess of color on her wall had broken through whatever block Jasmine had created in her mind, whatever was there telling her she wasn't artistic, that she wasn't creative.

When she had returned to school a few weeks later, she was the first to sign up when the theater department needed volunteers to create and paint scenery for their next production. She was at the top of the list whenever volunteers were needed for a creative project, and after a few months of that, she even had the courage to enroll in another art class. And luckily for her, Ms. Miller was much more encouraging of her creativity than her previous art teachers ever had been.

She took Cheddar out of the backpack, smiling as he began to explore the apartment. Gator, the senior tabby cat who lived with Viola, shot a look of betrayal at Jasmine before stalking away from the orange ball of energy that was currently chasing its tail with all the speed and intensity of a Tasmanian devil.

"I know, Gator," said Jasmine as she scratched behind his ears. "But he didn't have anywhere else to go. And I know you'll be a good role model for him. *Clearly*, he needs a little bit of direction."

She felt a pang of guilt for the older cat, for not making this transition as graceful as she *knew* you were supposed to. If she shared a video of this interaction on her Instagram account, the "experts" would come out in droves to tell her to introduce the two cats slowly, in different rooms, letting them smell each other through a closed door for days or even weeks before bringing them into the same space.

Thankfully, though, Gator was the feline equivalent of a Zen master, adept at navigating the behavioral idiosyncrasies of the wildest kitten. It helped that he often accompanied her to Kedi Cafe and was already acquainted with Cheddar from his workplace.

The look he was giving her now, though, spoke volumes. *I took* one *day off work and you brought* this *home to me? This is what happens when I take a personal day?*

"Sorry, bud," said Jasmine with a sheepish smile. "He'll settle down eventually, I'm sure. You know how kittens are...they're just a blur of energy and mayhem until they pass out and you actually get a moment of peace. At least we don't have any curtains here for him to shred."

She went in search of Cheddar then, a suspicious thudding sound emanating from the bathroom in the direction he had vanished just a moment prior. Entering the room, she found him perched in the sink, smacking at his own reflection in the mirror above, knocking first her toothpaste and then her moisturizer off the shelf with each movement of his paw.

Jasmine swooped in to grab Cheddar, stopping him just before his next swing could take out the glass jar where she kept her toothbrush. "Right. Thanks for the reminder that I need to kitten-proof the apartment." She took him out of the bathroom, closing the door behind her as she deposited him on her bed. "For now, at least, let's just keep you out of the bathroom. There's less trouble to get into here."

As soon as the words were out of her mouth, she felt a wave of doubt wash over her. With Cheddar's orange kitten energy, she had total confidence that he could—and would—uncover any opportunity to wreak mayhem in her apartment. Gone were the days when she could leave a dirty pot soaking on the kitchen counter or a discarded outfit tossed at the foot of her bed. Sure, Gator was trustworthy to a fault. But Cheddar? She could already visualize holes chewed in her socks, garbage cans emptied all over the kitchen floor, and the cat swinging from a chandelier, surveying his artwork.

"Thank goodness we don't have any chandeliers, then," said Jasmine out loud as she made her way back to the combined kitchen and living area, Cheddar on and around and between her heels. He cut in front of her just as she entered the room, leaping from the ground to the back of the couch, where Gator welcomed him with a soft hiss. "We're going to have fun together, the three of us," she said, with a pang of bittersweetness. It wasn't the same as having her grandmother here, staying in her home with one cat who had been her constant companion and another who was a chaos monster. But she needed the chaos, the noise, the activity to keep her from being alone with her thoughts, to keep her from being aware of just how much she would love to feel like she belonged somewhere.

Two

After a nearly sleepless night—letting Cheddar sleep on the foot of her bed next to Gator was a lost cause, and the alternative of kicking him out of her bedroom to have free rein of the rest of the apartment was just asking for trouble—Jasmine was back at the cat colony, dropping off food before the start of a new work day. Cheddar was once again in the space age backpack on her back, and he wasn't hesitating to voice his displeasure at being enclosed.

"Cheddar, you've got to cut it out," hissed Jasmine. "Someone is going to think a cat is being tortured and…I don't know, call the police?" At the sound of an approving chirp, she shook her head. "Oh, that's what you want, is it? Well sorry to tell you, honeybun, but I don't think Istanbul has cat police or cat lawyers in a cat court of law. No one is going to rule the backpack as cruel and unusual punishment, and, in fact, they're probably going to think it's pretty sweet and nice of me—or some of them might think it's idiotic and naïve of me—to carry you around like this."

"Why can't it be a little bit of all the above?" a deep voice came from behind the houses where the cats slept.

"Uh..." Jasmine stopped in her tracks, no longer moving towards the source of the voice. Sure, she was sleep deprived. But that didn't tend to manifest as hearing deep, sexy voices coming out of tiny tom cats, did it?

But before she could ask, a figure materialized behind the cat house, a man coming to a standing position from a crouch, where he had apparently been scattering food or scratching a belly, judging by the meowing cats who were now forming a cyclone around his ankles.

"You're not a cat," blurted Jasmine, feeling her cheeks color.

The man cocked his head at her. "I most certainly am not. Human, in fact. Just like you, I believe?"

She nodded back, then turned in profile so that he could see Cheddar in his backpack. "I am. This one's a cat, though. That's who I was talking to, not you. I didn't even know you were there. I thought..."

"You thought my voice was coming from a cat?" His face had split in a grin, and he was close enough that she could see his eyes crinkling at the corners. "Well, I think you either need to get some sleep because clearly you're dreaming, or else...coffee?" He said the last word as a question, raising both the tone of his voice and an eyebrow.

"Oh, coffee is definitely a necessity," said Jasmine with a nod. "I'm heading to work now to remedy the situation. It's pretty dire, you know. If I don't get my mind right and spend the day thinking cats are talking to me in sexy man voices, then I'm apt to fully lose my mind by the end of the day. If there was ever a city that should have a facility specifically for cat-related psychosis, it should be Istanbul, right? Strictly based on the size of the cat population, I mean. I'm not suggesting that anyone else in this city has this specific ailment…" She was rambling, she knew it. But as soon as the word "sexy" had slipped from the recesses of her mind and out her lips, dialing it down had been impossible. Perhaps the longer she kept talking, the less likely this stranger would be to pick up on what she had called him—or rather, his voice.

"Anyway," she continued, moving so quickly to disperse the food she had brought for the cats that she spilled it all around the bowls, far more kibble on the sidewalk than in the bowls, still calling over her shoulder to the man. "I should be out of here. Got to get to work. And to the coffee. Sorry for disturbing you."

"Wait." That voice stopped her in her tracks. "You didn't disturb me, quite the opposite. And I believe I invited you for a cup of coffee, if that would be agreeable to you."

She turned to him, sputtering. "You…invited me? I'm pretty sure you just suggested that I see to caffeinating myself as soon as possible before I continue embarrassing myself in front of handsome strangers." She clapped a hand over her mouth, shaking her head once. Then she turned to show him her profile again, with Cheddar in his backpack, suspiciously quiet now. "Plus, I've got this jerk with me. Can't exactly take him into a cafe with me, now can I?"

"Well, no. But I'm sure he would be welcome at Kedi Cafe, would he not? I haven't been in there myself, but from the name and reputation I would be surprised if they turned away any cats turning up for coffee." He exhaled a small laugh with a soft head shake. "It would be a first for me, visiting that cafe. Likely a last, too, unless it defies all of my expectations of such a place. I gather from the fact that you are speaking English that you aren't from around here. So maybe cat cafes and things like that don't seem quite as strange to you as they do to me, but..." He trailed off, a frown wrinkling his forehead. "What is it?"

"Kedi Cafe is my cafe. My grandmother's, actually, but it's mine at the moment." She jutted out her chin, ready to spin on her heel away from this man for the last time. "And I'm glad it doesn't appeal to you. We certainly aren't looking to appeal to the masses, just to the cat lovers. And if you're so against the idea of having a cup of coffee while a cute cat sleeps next to you, then I'm sure you can find a different place to sit and feel better than everyone else."

And with that, she was gone, ready to never see that man again. She didn't even turn back to see how her burn had landed on him, so sure was she that she had ended him with just a few sentences.

Three

J asmine spent the morning aggressively washing dishes, even ones that didn't need it. How dare that man insult her precious cafe, this piece of her beloved grandmother? Who even did that, carried on about how much they hated a place without first bothering to see if the person they were speaking to shared their opinion?

"That jerk, that's who." She shoved the Turkish tea glass she was rinsing into the drying rack, looking down at her feet to see Cheddar blinking up at her, his head cocked to the side.

"What are you...?" she began, trailing off as her eyes tracked the cat's pupils growing in size. Was he listening that intently to what she was saying? Was this cat, perhaps, a human who had been cursed to live as a cat, and he understood every word she was saying? Or were his eyes simply tracking the movement of the tassels on the hem of her shirt?

"Ouch!" she cried, as the cat's nails sank into the thin fabric of her yoga pants. Cheddar had launched himself at the hem of her shirt, his teeth on the tassels and all four of his feet—including every single one of his kitten-sharp claws—were digging into her right thigh.

"Get off!" she yelled, to no avail. Cheddar was lost in a world of shirt tassels, and Jasmine was seconds away from dropping the glasses and mugs in her hands and adding broken ceramic and glass to the mix.

It was the perfect moment for the doorbell of Kedi Cafe to chime, announcing the arrival of a customer. "Be with you in a sec!" she called over her shoulder through gritted teeth, shaking her leg now to release the offending beast.

The movement only seemed to trigger another level of ginger demon chaos monster madness in Cheddar, either because he was in danger of losing his grip on her leg or because the tassels were shaking even more frantically. Jasmine let out a shriek, then muffled it with her hand, hissing at the cat to release his grip.

It was a known fact in the cat cafe world that outwardly expressing anything that suggested one of the cafe's feline residents was anything less than docile and calm, all purrs and zero claws, was frowned upon. So Jasmine persisted, suffering in near silence, painfully aware of the customer who must now be at the counter, within view of her back.

"It looks like you could use some help there," said a vaguely familiar voice, a large physical presence approaching quickly after ducking behind the counter.

Jasmine turned and her jaw dropped at the sight of the man from the cat colony. "You!" she spat at him, shaking her head. "What are you doing here? I thought this place didn't meet your standards."

He rolled his eyes at her, crouching down in front of her leg. "May I help you free yourself from this unfortunate situation before I answer that question?"

"Fine," she said through gritted teeth, wishing her hands were free so she could cross them over her chest.

The man gave a quick nod, said something to the cat in Turkish, placed one hand on the scruff of the kitten's neck, and used the other to extricate his claws, the whole thing resulting in Jasmine being cat-free in about seven seconds.

She set the glasses and mugs in her hands on the counter, massaging her sore thigh with one hand. "Wow, uh...thanks," she said to the man. "That was quick. Where were you two minutes ago when that little monster first climbed my leg like a tree trunk?"

He gave a small smile, still holding the cat in his arms. Cheddar was purring now, but his eyes were trained on the hem of Jasmine's shirt. "I got here as soon as I could," said the man. "I think, though, that you're going to have to take off your shirt."

Jasmine's hands flew to cover her chest, her stomach. "Excuse me? What, you think that just because you helped me out, now I owe you...what? A peep show? To bring some fantasy to life of having coffee served to you topless?"

His face had flushed red, and he was shaking his head. "No," he said, quite firmly. He tilted his head towards the cat, whose pupils had grown wide, a sure sign that danger was coming. "But this guy definitely has a fantasy of attacking those tassels at the hem of your shirt, and if you don't change it, you're going to spend the day with him pouncing on your legs."

"Ah," she replied, feeling the heat in her own cheeks to match his. If she had embarrassed him with her accusation, the karma was instant because she was mortified, wishing to drop through the floor of the cafe and sink all the way down to the center of the earth. "Gotcha. Um..." She looked around behind the counter, willing a spare shirt that she already knew didn't exist to materialize. Her eyes landed on an apron, and she made short work of wrapping it around her waist to conceal the tassels, before tying the strings into a knot behind her and tucking them away and out of Cheddar's sight.

"That's the best I can do for now," she said with a sigh. "But I'm burning this shirt when I go home."

The man smiled then, giving Cheddar one more scratch under his chin before placing him on the floor. The animal bounded away, pouncing on an older cat who was sleeping like a loaf in a sunny spot near the window.

Jasmine shook her head at his antics. "Thanks again," she said to the man, forcing a small smile. "I appreciate the help and the heads up about the shirt. And you holding him back so he didn't just do the same thing again as soon as he was on the ground."

"I'm just glad I was here to offer some assistance," said the man. "Though I suppose it would have been better for you if I had been here just a bit sooner."

She gave him a small smile. "It's okay, really. I'm sure I'll live, and I doubt I'll even have a cool scar to show for it."

His lips lifted in a sheepish approximation of a smile. "I didn't just come here to rescue you from that cat, though." A hand came up to rub the back of his neck, his eyes dropping from hers to track Cheddar's movements at her feet. "I wanted to clarify...er, to apologize, I suppose, for the misunderstanding this morning." He gestured around them to the cafe. "I have nothing against your cafe, and I am truly sorry that it came across as disparaging. I haven't actually tried your coffee yet—hoping to remedy that here shortly—but for all intents and purposes, it seems to be a great business with a unique idea."

Jasmine frowned. "So what's the problem, then? Because it sure didn't come across that way when you were talking about it just a few moments ago."

He grimaced. "It's not about you. It's, well...it's about the cats."

She felt her eyes goggle at him, practically bulging from her face. "Make that make sense. You were the one at the cat colony this morning, feeding all those strays before I even got there. And you certainly knew your way around Cheddar when he was climbing my leg like a tree trunk." She placed her hands on her hips. "Not to mention the fact that you live in Istanbul, of all places. Are you really going to tell me that you live in what could probably be called the capital of the cat kingdom and you...what? Don't like them?"

"It's not that I don't like them. Come on, I'm not a monster. I have enjoyed every cat I have ever met, and feeding strays gives my days purpose and meaning."

She crossed her arms over her chest. "Oh, I'm just *fascinated* how you're going to come back from that. You can't say that cats give your life purpose and meaning and then not want to be around them. It doesn't make sense."

"I like them in their place. I want to be around them in appropriate contexts. And as much as I can understand cats being a part of the scenery of Istanbul—and I'm even happy to drop a piece of meat from my dinner on the ground at an outdoor restaurant to share with one." He shot a meaningful look in the direction of Cheddar, who was chasing a piece of plastic around behind the counter. "But you can't deny that, when it comes to business, at least, they add a level of chaos that can be nearly impossible to manage."

"That is absurd. You know that, right?" Jasmine scoffed, shaking her head in disbelief. "You mean to tell me that, rather than going with the flow of life, working around the cats who cross your path, you...would prefer they go someplace else and give you some peace and quiet? What do you do, anyway, that's so disrupted by cats and their chaos?"

"I'm a real estate developer."

"Ha!" Jasmine's laugh barked out of her before she could second guess it. "So you're really doing the important work, huh?"

He pursed his lips. "Well, I would think building affordable, earthquake-safe homes for the residents of Istanbul is important, but if you disagree..."

"Of course I don't disagree." She could feel heat flushing her cheeks anew. "I just don't see how cats would be such a problem. Are they messing up your construction site or something?"

"Well, that's the thing. We haven't actually broken ground yet, because the site in question is where the colony you and I visited this morning is located."

She felt her eyes widen with comprehension. "I see. So...what? What are you going to do with the cats there?"

"Whether you believe it or not, I don't just want to destroy their home, leave them in search of a safe place to live, or, more likely to get into fights with other cats when they inevitably start encroaching on their territory." He gave a small shrug. "I'm open to suggestions, actually. I went there this last night to feed them for the first time and then again this morning, hoping to, I don't know...get to know them? Hope that a solution presents itself?"

Jasmine was quiet, nodding along with his words. It was a more compassionate question than she had expected him to broach. "I'm happy to hear that. You could have just shooed them away, treated the consequences as if they weren't your fault, had nothing to do with you." She bit the inside of her lower lip. "I'll admit that no easy solutions come to mind. But if there's anything I can do to help, then I absolutely will."

His eyes brightened, the corners of his lips turning up in a smile. "Really? That would be amazing. Maybe we could scout out a new location for them together. Or...I don't know...hold an adoption event here? I don't know how these things work."

"I...don't really either." For all her bluster and the frustration she had directed at him, Jasmine wasn't exactly an expert in the social dynamics of cats. Sure, she understood it on a smaller scale, like introducing Cheddar and Gator, but when it came to the relocation of entire communities, she found herself at a bit of a loss. "I could ask my vet for some advice." She shrugged. "He should know more about these kinds of things, shouldn't he?"

The man nodded slowly. "I guess so. Would it be alright with you if we both met with him?"

Jasmine narrowed her eyes. "Why? Don't trust that I can handle it myself?"

"No, of course, that's not it. I just...well, to be honest, this is my first major development project, and I'm really trying to do things right. Keep my finger on all the pulses, as it were. And even if you don't believe me, I do care about those cats and I do want to make sure this is handled in the most appropriate way."

"Ah. So you want to make sure nothing shady goes down behind the scenes that you end up getting raked over the coals for in the future?"

"I...what? No!" He sputtered, and Jasmine laughed.

"I'm just kidding, dude, relax. Pretty sure that sort of extreme scrutiny is reserved for people with a little more clout than a real estate developer. I mean, you aren't some famous actor who's just dabbling in real estate, are you? Should I know who you are?"

"I can't think of any reason why you would. I'm Burak," he said, extending his hand.

She took it in her own, feeling his warm, firm grasp. "Jasmine," she replied. "And that's Cheddar." She released his hand to jerk her thumb in the direction of the orange beast, who was eyeballing the curtain. Jasmine marched over to him and scooped him up just as his haunches started wiggling, seconds before he was sure to launch himself into the curtains yet again. "And we clearly need to figure out a different way to provide sun protection in here. I don't suppose there are any real estate development secrets for that, are there?"

That got Burak's attention. "Well, if it isn't an option to keep the cat away from the curtains, then outside, perhaps—"

"It's not an option," she interrupted.

He nodded. "Right, that's as I expected. You could try blinds, though you might run into a similar problem. You could add a window tint or perhaps an awning outside would do the trick for the vast majority of the daylight hours."

"Hmm." She considered his words with a small nod. "Well, I'll file those ideas away on my list of things to do if I ever have an excess of cash lying around and am looking for a project to burn it on." She forced her lips into a small smile shot in his direction. He *had* tried to help, after all. "I appreciate the suggestions, though. Probably should have mentioned we were talking about a project with a zero dollar budget."

"I could help." The words escaped his lips, seemingly without his awareness that they were about to do so, judging by the shocked expression that followed their exit.

"You...why? Why would you even suggest that? Surely you're busy enough with your cat eviction project." She turned her back on him and set to washing some mugs that were already clean. If she didn't keep her hands busy, there was no telling what they might do.

"It would be no big deal, I promise. I can get the materials for an awning at wholesale cost, and it won't take long to put it up. It'll be a way for me to thank you for your help with the colony. I don't know if you could tell when you found me there this morning, but cats aren't exactly my area of expertise and I feel pretty in over my head with this particular project."

"Hmm." She focused her attention on scrubbing nonexistent stains from the bottom of the mug in her hands. "You seemed to handle Cheddar just fine."

"Sure, but a whole colony? That's different. It would mean the world to me to have a partner helping me figure this out. Making sure we do right by the cats."

"I've already said I'll help with that." Her words came out more abruptly than she had intended.

"Okay, then…" She could hear the hesitation in his voice. "Then what exactly is the problem with me returning the favor by getting an awning set up here for you?"

Jasmine dropped the soapy mug in the sink and whirled to face him again, water flying from her fingertips. What exactly *was* the problem? And how could she put it into words, even if she knew what the issue was? "I'm just not crazy about getting into weird reciprocal relationships with strange men. I'm happy to help with the cats and leave it at that. We barely even need to be in each other's lives, so you certainly don't need to be coming around here taking measurements and installing awnings."

"I see." His smile was small and sad as he gave her a single nod. "I respect your need for space and the boundaries you've established. I won't feel right about taking your time and energy unless I'm able to return the favor in this way, so can I promise to do that in the way that will be the least invasive? I promise to stay out of your hair, to spend as little time here as necessary, and I won't even speak to you if you don't want me to."

She frowned as she crossed her arms over her chest, immediately regretting the move as her wet hands soaked through the sides of her shirt. "I'm not sure if you're mocking me by taking my words to such extremes, but—"

"Absolutely not," he interjected. "I am simply respecting your boundaries."

"Okay, well, at ease, soldier. Or...down, boy. Whichever term you prefer, I guess." She exhaled a sigh that conveyed a level of exhaustion with the whole situation that surprised her. "I mean, yes. Please. I would love to have the curtain situation resolved. And I understand that you feel like you need to do something nice for me too, so...yeah. Let's do the thing."

"Great," said Burak, a smile spreading across his face. "I have a feeling this is the beginning of a beautiful partnership." His eyes landed on an old photo of Viola and Jasmine next to the sink, and something like recognition flashed in his eyes.

Jasmine rolled her eyes, then went back to rinsing the mug she had already washed three times. "Don't get carried away, bud. We'll be out of each other's hair before you know it."

Four

Jasmine was still fuming from her interactions with Burak when the cafe's bell jingled to announce the arrival of a customer. "I'll be right with you!" she called, from where she was ducking down to fill the pastry case with freshly baked poğaça and simit, just dropped off by the delivery boy from the bakery down the block.

"Take your time," said a familiar voice, bringing a smile to Jasmine's face and forcing her to her feet instantly.

"Celia!" she cried as she came around to the front of the counter to pull the woman into a hug. "It's so good to see you! Are you back now?"

Celia was a fellow expat, and Jasmine had met her months prior, when her grandmother was still around. In early days of her stay in Istanbul, Jasmine had forced herself out of the house in search of some much-needed connection. She had run into Celia—and her partner, Enes, who was now Jasmine's vet—on one such occasion, braving a meetup hosted by a local expat group in Taksim. The expat group hadn't stuck—neither woman had gone to one of their events before or since—but a connection between Celia and Jasmine had been cemented that day.

Celia was nodding. "I just got back last night, so I'm going to be taking my coffee intravenously today, I think. Jet lag is no joke."

"Oh you poor thing. You should have just stayed home and slept today. I could have delivered coffee." Celia had returned from a visit to her family in St. Louis, where she had been for the last two weeks. "I bet Enes is glad you're back."

Celia's smile at the mention of her boyfriend was so genuine, so warm, that Jasmine had to look away. It felt like she was intruding on a private moment, seeing unguarded emotion like that. "Oh, he definitely is. Badem is too, though I think the two of them bonded so much while I was gone that she hardly missed me."

Badem was the cat Celia had rescued (or been rescued by, depending on who you asked) her first day in Istanbul and one of the main reasons she had decided to set down roots in the city. Of course, Enes had played his role in that, too.

And judging by the way Badem had looked at Celia on the occasions that Jasmine had been invited to the apartment she and Enes shared, there was *no* chance the space Celia occupied in her cat's heart had been filled by anyone else. Badem could teach Cheddar and Gator a thing or two about making their human feel special. Didn't they know the ultimate secret to feline bliss was manipulating human emotions with tail chasing and *Puss in Boots* eyes until you got every single thing you ever wanted?

Jasmine set about preparing a fresh mug of coffee for her friend, nodding towards the best table in the cafe. Celia looked grateful and relieved as she nearly collapsed into her chair, her hands coming out to encircle the mug as soon as Jasmine deposited it, taking the seat across from her.

"So," she began, "how was everything?"

Celia took a long sip of coffee, closed her eyes, and let a slow smile spread across her face. "Exhausting. But that was just the travel. The trip itself was great, being back around the whole family. Eating all my favorite foods, of both the home cooked and the international restaurant variety. But as great as it was to be there, it's even better to be back. This really feels like home now, you know?" She traced the handle of the mug. "It has for a while, but this is the longest I've been gone since Enes and I moved in together."

Jasmine felt her eyebrows climb her forehead. "No kidding? Well, I'd say that's a win. Good thing you didn't discover that you actually liked living alone better than having him as a roomie." As soon as the words were out, she cringed. "I don't know why I said that. Enes is a great guy, and of course the two of you are happy together." She sucked her lower lip into her mouth. "Actually, I might know why I said that. It's possible I'm just anti-man today, and the thought of having to live with one sounds like my actual worst nightmare."

That got a reaction out of Celia. Her brow quirked upward, and her mouth formed the perfect shape of surprise. "Okay, that got my attention. Spill. Did you get cat called today or something? Is there a skull I need to crush?"

Jasmine stared at her friend. "Wow, jet lag makes you violent. And also possibly inclined to overestimate the strength of those twigs you call arms…" She reached across the table, where Celia was flexing a bicep and glaring at her with indignation. "Okay, you proved me wrong. Those are *definitely* skull crushing muscles." She sighed as she pulled back her hand. "But no, I don't think I need to call in your favors of violence and mayhem. Not yet, anyway. Do you know some real estate guy named Burak?"

Celia leveled a stare at her that made Jasmine snort with laughter. "You're right, that was an absurd question. There are 15 million people in this city, so what are the odds you know some guy I met this morning?"

"Right. And you aren't even giving me a last name? Please." She took a sip of her coffee. "Where did you meet him? Did he come here to ask about the building? Are you selling Kedi Cafe?" She blinked twice in quick succession. "Is jet lag making me jump to bizarre conclusions?"

Jasmine paused to think for a moment. "Well, I'll admit I've never seen you like this. Though I have a feeling if I had known you when we were teenagers and we had pulled an all-nighter hyped up on sugar and rom coms, I would have seen this side of you. Lots of giggling, the origin of lots of inside jokes that would keep us laughing for years, even if they never made even one bit of sense."

"Hmm." Celia nodded. "It does feel a bit like that, I guess. For what it's worth, I'm happy to laugh with you about my muscular biceps and Burak Whats-His-Name for as long as we both shall live."

"Sounds great." Warmed from within at something her friend had said, Jasmine smiled. It wasn't as if her future in Istanbul was certain—Grandma would return from her cruise, after all, and everything after that was a question mark. Would she stay in the city, make her own home here? Or would it be time to move on? Either way, the likelihood of her friendship with Celia being a lifelong one felt far from a certainty, and it was bittersweet to imagine their blossoming inside jokes fading away until even the memory of each other's faces had vanished.

"Right," she said, clearing her throat. "So, Burak wasn't here about buying the cafe or knocking down the building or anything like that. I bumped into him at the cat colony this morning—you know, the one over by the vacant lot? I've been feeding those guys for a while."

"Was he feeding them, too?" At Jasmine's nod, Celia reciprocated the gesture. "Right, so that's a positive mark for him then. We love a man who looks out for all catkind."

"*We* do? I know *you* certainly do, but I just met Burak, and it wasn't love at first sight."

Celia's wave was dismissive. "What happened next?"

"Oh, you know...just a classic misunderstanding. And then he turned up here and pulled Cheddar's claws out of my thigh and now he wants my help to relocate the colony and in return he's going to do some light remodeling to the cafe free of charge."

Celia blinked slowly, then again. "Am I hearing you correctly, or are my ears still messed up from the flight? This guy gave you a thigh massage and now he wants to do free work around the cafe?"

Jasmine nodded. "More or less. *Less* of a massage and *more* of a kitten extraction. And the free labor would be in return for my help with the cat colony."

"Is this a scam?" Celia narrowed her eyes at Jasmine. "Is there some expectation that you will wire him money? Or did he claim that he's royalty? Or...help me out here. I'm not that familiar with the current scams going around."

"There's no exchange of money, so don't worry about that. And it's not as if he's going to knock down walls and build an extension or anything. We were just troubleshooting what to do about the curtains, since Cheddar insists on climbing them. Burak is going to install an awning."

"Ah." Celia gave a knowing nod. "So that's it, then. 'Burak is going to install an awning,' she says, as if it's the most normal thing in the world for a total stranger to do."

Through gritted teeth, Jasmine responded. "Look, I know it all sounds sketchy. And trust me, I'm far from sold on the idea of this guy being my personal genie or anything like that. Why don't I introduce you to him?" She rushed to clarify. "I don't mean on like a double date or something...we're going to need to talk to Enes at some point, get his guidance with the whole cat colony thing. You should be there too. See if you can suss him out, read his aura, or get a feel for his vibes, or whatever it is that you need to do in order to figure out if he's a good dude."

Celia looked skeptical. "Well, that isn't even up for debate. Of course I'm going to meet him." She scoffed. "Especially if it's you and Enes making the decision on his character. You two aren't exactly known for being discerning when it comes to meeting new people."

Jasmine raised an eyebrow. "That sounds like a very concerning thing to hear you say about the man you live with. The love of your life. The co-parent of your cat."

Celia sniffed. "Obviously, I was the exception. Plus, he had Badem to vouch for my character, and we all know she's got the best taste in humans around."

Jasmine nodded, but didn't say anything in response. No matter what happened, it could be fun to get all four of them together in a room. And hopefully by the end of it, she would know what to think about Burak.

Five

It was only when Celia was gone that Jasmine realized she had no way of actually getting in contact with Burak, that she could only wait and hope he would appear again if they were going to make arrangements to meet Enes and Celia together.

She didn't have to wait long. As she was preparing to close the cafe for the evening, the door chimed again, announcing the arrival of a customer. Jasmine looked up from the table she was bussing, hoping that whoever was about to grace her counter would keep their order simple enough so she could head home as soon as possible. It had been a good day but a long one, and she was ready to curl up on her couch with a glass of wine and Gator. If Cheddar wanted to join them—if he promised to keep calm and carry on and not stick his paws in her glass—then he was certainly welcome to do so.

When Jasmine's eyes landed on Burak, she felt a thrill of anticipation run through her. *No, that couldn't be right,* she thought. *It must be anticipation of the excitement of arguing with him. There couldn't be any other reason for her to be happy to see him.*

And yet, as he walked closer to her, his own face splitting wide with a smile, she couldn't help but smile back as she rose to her full height from the table she had been wiping, her eyes coming level with his.

"Good evening, Jasmine," he said, his deep voice vibrating in her belly. "I was hoping I would catch you before you left."

"And that you did," she replied, shifting the tub full of dirty dishes onto her hip and turning to the kitchen.

Burak took the hint and followed her, falling into step beside her. "I hope you had a good day. And I hope that, like me, you've only gotten more convinced that the two of us have work to do together. That we would make a great team."

She stopped and faced him, her lips pursed. "How would I know that the two of us would make a great team? Apart from your name and the fact that you're a real estate developer, I don't know a thing about you."

With a wrinkled eyebrow, he studied her. "I'd say you know a little more than that. I *did* rescue you from your own beast of a cat, after all." Cheddar, as if sensing that he was the topic of discussion, meowed in greeting and pranced over to twine himself around Burak's legs.

Jasmine shrugged. "Anyone would have done that." She sniffed, turning back to continue her journey to the kitchen. "But I do agree about the colony, the work we need to do. I spoke with my vet's girlfriend and was actually just thinking about how to get in touch with you so that all of us could meet up."

Burak nodded, bending down to scoop up Cheddar into his arms. He flipped the cat quickly onto his back, petting his belly as the traitorous animal began to purr. Jasmine looked away from the sight that was stirring up uncomfortable and unwelcome feelings.

"So you're setting us up on a double date with your vet? I have to admit, I didn't expect that, exactly, but I'm game if you are."

"It's not a double date," she replied through gritted teeth. "His girlfriend is my friend, and I told her about the need for a meeting about the colony. It was only natural to include her, considering that I'm friends with both of them."

Burak's grin conveyed that he was pleased with himself to a level that made her nervous. Had she said something wrong? "What?" she asked, narrowing her eyes at him.

"I'm just tickled to learn that you were speaking to your friend about me. You must have shared some intriguing opinions about me for her to decide instantly to have a double date to size me up." He stood a little taller then, adjusting his arms—and the cat in them—in a way that suggested he just might be flexing his muscles.

Jasmine rolled her eyes and huffed out a laugh. "That *does* seem like the kind of conclusion you would jump to, just based on my vast knowledge of you and your character." As soon as the words were out, she wanted to recall them. There was a difference between a good-natured ribbing and needlessly criticizing someone who had, in fact, only been a partial source of annoyance since she had met him. There was plenty that he had done that was perfectly pleasant, even generous and kind. Still, why was there a part of her that wanted to tease him for every word out of his mouth?

Her stomach dropped with horror as a realization dawned on her. Was this like the feeling that had fueled her teenage crushes, making her say and do things that her rational mind couldn't explain?

Is there something about a crush that makes teasing an inevitability? Like, something evolutionary? she wondered, making a mental note to look it up later. For now, at least, she could extend just a crumb of kindness to Burak, ignoring the fact that her subconscious mind had all but told her she had a crush on the man.

She repressed a shiver at the thought and smiled as she turned to face Burak. "Anyway," she continued, "Enes and Celia are some of my best friends in Istanbul—and he just so happens to be my vet, too. There's no need to deprive you of the pleasure of meeting Celia by trying to keep things strictly business with Enes. If I'm going to meet him—if *we're* going to meet him—then she should be there, too. And if it turns into dinner and drinks as well, then I really don't see anything wrong with that."

Burak nodded, but there was a mischievous smile playing at the corner of his mouth. "I don't think there's anything wrong with it, either. Just like I don't think there's anything wrong with admitting that you want to go on a double date with me. Show me off to your friends or get their opinion on me before we take things further. I don't know exactly what your motivation is there, but I'm on board no matter what."

Jasmine gaped at him. "Did you forget to wear your hard hat today? And did, oh I don't know, a *piano* fall off of one of your construction sites and land on your head?" She put a hand on her hip as she tilted her chin down to study him from a different angle. "Are you secretly a cartoon character?"

But he kept that same smug smile on his face as he shook his head. "None of those things. Why do you ask?"

"I just..." She set the tray of dishes down on the counter, then flung her hands up in exasperation. "Where did this come from, this sudden confidence that I want to date you? It's not as if we have a long and storied history, sir, and I don't believe there's ever been any indication of taking our...er...*acquaintanceship* to the next level." She shook her head. "Actually, scratch that. We *did* talk about taking our acquaintanceship to the next level of working together. But that doesn't explain any of *this*." She gestured between them. "You had better start making sense soon, or else the whole thing is going to be off."

"The whole thing? You wouldn't even let me go on our double date?" Burak grimaced as she crossed her arms over her chest, then he lightly set Cheddar on the floor. When he came back to his full height, he held up his hands as if to assure her that he was unarmed. "You're right. There has, perhaps, been a sudden and sharp increase in flirty behavior on my behalf. I should...explain? Would that help?"

"It most definitely would. And whatever you say determines whether I kick you right out of here or help you sort out all your cat troubles, so...you know. No pressure..."

"Right." With a resolute nod, Burak rubbed his hands together.

He had the decency to look slightly sheepish, and as that awareness crossed Jasmine's mind, she felt a wave of anxiety rush over her. "What?" she asked, before he could even begin to explain. "This feels weirdly sinister. Did someone put you up to this?"

His eyes widened. "Not exactly, but...wow. You're pretty on the nose." Off the look on her face, he rushed to explain. "I know your grandmother. The woman in the picture in the kitchen. I didn't know you were her granddaughter when I met you, not until I came here and saw that and figured it out. We go to the same bakery. Chatted in line there at least a few times every week."

Jasmine gawked at him. Why did his knowing her grandmother make her feel so exposed? Perhaps the more important question was, what had Viola told him about her that she would prefer he didn't know?

The only way to find out was to ask. "And what, once you stopped laughing about me performing in the school talent show with my skirt tucked into my underwear, you decided to come here and torment me right to my face?"

"Believe it or not, no. If you're concerned that your grandmother shared all your embarrassing stories with me, let me reassure you that she did not. I'd never heard of you performing in the talent show with your underwear on display until just now, and while I see how it could be humorous to some, I hope you'll notice and appreciate that I am, in fact, not laughing. I'm sorry that happened to you, actually."

"Then what?" Jasmine's cheeks were flushing with the awareness that she had blurted her most embarrassing experience to this near-stranger, and she looked around for something to busy herself with to get some blood out of her face and back into other parts of her body. Why, oh why, was she so good at cleaning up as the day went along? If only she had a mountain of dishes, rather than a couple of loose mugs...

Burak's hand fell on her forearm, the pressure gentle and his touch surprisingly warm. "Jasmine," he said, and so help her, she loved the way her name sounded rolling off his tongue. "When I understood that you were Ms. Viola's granddaughter, I believe I crossed some wires in my head and that came out in the way I was speaking to you. I apologize for that. Your grandmother and I, we are pretty friendly. She always makes me laugh, and I try to return the favor. I think I brought that same energy here to you today and let it make me behave as if we are better friends than we actually are. I hope that, with time, we will become friends. In the meantime, if you don't want me to flirt with you, I will stop immediately."

The thought of that was surprisingly unwelcome, but Jasmine wasn't ready to examine that thought and certainly not to express it to Burak. So she did the only thing she could and played it off.

"You didn't flirt with my grandmother, did you? I mean, what is this? Am I somehow taking her place?" Jasmine shuddered at the thought. "If so, you know where the door is."

"Your grandmother and I were friends, Jasmine. *Friends.* Nothing more and nothing less." He chuckled then. "I showed her Turkish hospitality, but I certainly didn't flirt with her. You know as well as I do that she wouldn't have stood for it, not to mention the fact that she is totally and completely in love with Morty."

"That's true. It's disgusting." Jasmine shook her head. "I don't mean that. It's adorable, and I'm glad they found each other, and of *course* I'm glad she has a partner on her journey around the world. I think it comes with the territory of being single and jaded that you have to find other people's relationships at least slightly disgusting, even if you're actually really happy for them."

Burak tilted his head to the side, as if he were considering her words and acknowledging them, but was being careful not to imply that he agreed with them. "Perhaps," he finally said. "Though I have always found that feeling envy or jealousy for what someone else has that I do not is much more about me than it is about them. And if it pushes me to seek out or create that thing in my own life, then it only ends up bringing me happiness."

"I'm not jealous of Grandma and Morty."

"No?"

"Of course not." Jasmine wiped her hands on her jeans, returning to the already wiped tables to once again polish their surfaces. This conversation had just proven yet again that it would be best conducted alongside a task rather than receiving her undivided attention. "And forget what I said about being single and jaded. We weren't talking about me. We were talking about you and my grandmother and why you have suddenly become so...weird." She gestured to him to continue with her free hand. "So what now? Maybe you should just go and we can cancel this whole *thing* between us and forget all this weirdness ever happened."

"No, no. I don't want that." He held up a hand in protest, then moved forward to help her, traveling from table to table to straighten the sugar packets and salt and pepper shakers. "I'm sorry for not explaining myself sooner. After learning that you were *the* Jasmine that Ms. Viola always talked about, I was quite excited to see you again." He looked up from his work to give her a warm smile. "Your grandmother is so fond of you, Jasmine. I don't think a day went by that I didn't hear a story about you, and with every story that I heard, I was more convinced that I needed to meet you and that I would really like you when I did." His gaze dropped back to the table then. "Of course, it was also helped by the fact that your grandmother may have dropped hints—or perhaps *hint* isn't a strong enough word—that she would like to set the two of us up. But I digress—"

Jasmine dropped the cloth she was holding onto the table as she wheeled to face Burak. "Are you kidding me? My grandma just...what? Decided to set the two of us up with each other and only bothered to tell *you* about it?" She leaned back over the table, picked up the cloth, and started scrubbing at invisible stains with aggression. "Oh, she is going to hear about this. I was giving her space, letting her enjoy her cruise, not wanting to bother her with any of the day-to-day cafe-related things. But she is going to *hear* about this."

When she glanced at Burak over her shoulder, his gaze was down and his lips were a straight line, and Jasmine felt a softening towards him.

"This isn't your fault, Burak. And I'm not saying that, like...I'm so upset at the idea of being set up with you that I have to call her and berate her for it. It's more about neglecting to let me in on critical details. I'm not a fan of being kept in the dark."

"I absolutely understand that." He gave her a small smile. "And I do hope that we can be friends, even now that this is out in the open."

"I think it'll be easier to be friends now that we are both aware of the situation." She wiped her hands on her pants and took a step towards him. "Do you think you can dial down the flirtation? Keep things strictly friendly between us?"

"If that's what you want, then yes, of course." The smile he gave her didn't quite reach his eyes. "Naturally, though, if you change your mind and decide you *do* in fact want me to flirt with you, then by all means, please let me know."

That got a laugh out of Jasmine. "It's a deal." She held out a hand for him to shake, smiling as his warm fingers wrapped around hers. "Just to warn you, it's highly un-likely I'll be changing my mind about that anytime soon."

"A man can only hope." He winked at her, followed im-mediately by a visible cringe. "Sorry about that. I promise to get my eyes on board with the rest of me. No more winking."

"No more winking," she said, giving his hand one more shake before releasing her grip.

Six

When Jasmine returned to the apartment that evening, she barely had her shoes off before she was dialing her grandmother's phone number. Would she even have cell phone coverage? She hadn't checked the itinerary in about a week, so she had no idea where her grandmother was apt to be, how close she might be to land. Beyond that, she didn't know if it was an excursion day, a time when she was likely to be so busy enjoying herself that she wouldn't even hear her phone ring, if she even had it on her.

As the phone began to ring, she crouched down next to the cat backpack to release Cheddar, petting Gator at the same time as he twined around her legs. "I'll feed you boys in a minute," she promised the animals, before walking into the living room to stare out the window as the phone continued to ring.

She was just about to give up when her grandmother's voice came through the line, sounding tinny and distant. "Jasmine? Is that you?"

Jasmine sighed with relief at that familiar voice, her grandmother's accent so unlike her own and yet such a source of comfort and grounding. She was surprised by the emotion that welled up in her throat, nearly spilling out of her eyes.

That is, of course, until she remembered why she had called her grandmother. "Yes, it's me, Grandma. How's it going?" She fixed her lips in a line, already prepared for the scolding she would need to deliver once the pleasantries had been dispensed with.

"Oh, it's just lovely, Jasmine. I wish we could have brought you with us! You would just love St. Kitts. The weather has been absolutely gorgeous, and the *food*. Well, let's just say I could retire on board this ship and be happy as a clam."

"That's nice," said Jasmine, forcing a smile into her voice, though it was obvious to her why she hadn't been asked along on the cruise. If she weren't here to take care of the apartment, Gator, and the cafe, then what other plan did her grandmother have? Sure, it was a fortuitous ask for her, as she had been in need of somewhere to go and something to do, but that didn't mean she hadn't bailed out her grandmother at the same time.

"Is everything okay there? How are the cats? Give Gator a scratch for me. And how are you?"

"Everything is fine here, Grandma. Except...well, I guess there's no point beating around the bush. What in the world did you say to this Burak character about me?"

"Oh!" There was laughter in her grandmother's voice now. "You met Burak? That's wonderful. Isn't he just such a gem? I thought the two of you would get along famously, and I don't even need to ask, but don't you?"

Jasmine spoke through gritted teeth. "Tough to say. I just met him today, so the jury is still out as far as what I think about him. But imagine my surprise to learn that he apparently already knows *everything* about me, and as soon as he knew that I was your granddaughter, he turned on the charm and practically flirted my face off."

There was a pause. "I'm afraid I don't know what that means, dear. But why do you sound so upset? Burak is a lovely fellow, and I wouldn't have sung your praises to him if I didn't mean every word and if I didn't believe with all my heart that he was a good man."

A deep sigh escaped Jasmine's lips. "That is *so* not the point, Grandma."

"Then what is, dear? I'm having trouble following what's got you so upset."

Jasmine shook her head. Was her grandmother really that clueless, or was she actively manipulating her granddaughter? And was that granddaughter justified in being as frustrated as she felt, or was there a chance, perhaps, that she was overreacting?

Too late now to change tactics, she told herself. "It's the blindsiding, actually. It's the fact that this total stranger knew all about me and apparently already had your blessing to...what, *date* me? And I'd never even heard of him. I felt so exposed, Grandma. That was seriously uncool."

"I'm sorry if you didn't appreciate the surprise of it all, dear. I didn't consider that. But you have to remember that he's only a *total stranger*"—Jasmine could practically hear her grandmother making air quotes over those two words—"to you. To me, he's an old friend. I wouldn't have sung your praises to a stranger on the street."

"Okay, well..." Jasmine trailed off. What could she even say to that? With every word out of her grandmother's mouth, she felt more and more like there was a chance she was overreacting.

Until, that is, Viola spoke again.

"And as far as you not liking surprises, well, I'm afraid I didn't even consider that. I just imagined myself in your shoes, young and single and beautiful, and the idea of someone older and wiser playing matchmaker for me felt, frankly, exciting." It sounded like Viola was barely holding herself back from giggling. "If anything, you should be thanking me, dear. Or perhaps that comes later, once you realize just what a wonderful gift it is that I've given you."

"Uh uh. No way." Jasmine stared at her reflection in the glass, giving herself a "is she serious? She *can't* be serious" eyebrow raise as she shook her head. "First of all, it doesn't work that way, even if you want it to. And second of all, do you really think that my life is so sad and empty that I'm just dying to be introduced to the right man? If I'm going to thank you profusely for anything—which I have, time and time again, if you'll recall—it'll be for the opportunity to stay here. To be in Istanbul. To run the cafe. These are all life-changing things, Grandma, and I don't take them lightly." She sighed. "I just wish I didn't get the feeling that you believe I won't be happy unless I've got a man by my side."

"Jasmine." Viola's tone was stern, and Jasmine noted the use of her first name over the usual "dear" with alarm. "I never said that, and don't put words in my mouth. Goodness knows I've had plenty of experiences and successes that didn't revolve around relationships. I was happy with your grandfather, of course, but I managed to be happy again when he was gone. And I'm happy now with Morty. My happiness, just like yours, doesn't depend solely on the partner that's by my side."

Jasmine waited for the other shoe to drop.

"But just because you're a feminist and I'm a feminist and we could all burn our bras right now if we wanted to, does that mean that I should stop myself from sending you someone who just might happen to be your soulmate? Must I deprive you of that just...what? To make some kind of point about how it's not so bad being single?"

"Um." Jasmine's voice was small. "What do you mean, *soulmate*? I thought you just thought Burak was a nice young man. Handsome. Respectful, I assume. Or ambitious, or whatever."

Viola sighed. "Well, that's all I *intended* to tell you, yes. But then you got me all fired up, and I said some things I didn't mean to say." She paused for a beat before she continued. "But it's true. It's not just those surface level things that made me connect the dots and want you to meet Burak. There's something deeper there, I know it. Something that was practically begging me to get the two of you in the same room. Of course I was also trying not to scare you off in the process and I'm afraid I may have ruined that."

All of Jasmine's self righteousness deflated at her grandmother's words, replaced by something that felt more like anxiety. Her grandmother had expectations of what could—what *should*, as far as she was concerned—exist between Jasmine and Burak, and not only did it seem like she had already ruined it, but the idea of letting down both her grandmother and her future self's potential happiness was all too much.

"Will you do something for me?" Viola's voice sounded small, coming down the line. "Will you just...I don't know, give Burak, give *yourself* a chance?" She sighed. "I'm guessing from how quiet you got that you're causing yourself a great deal of stress right now, and that's exactly why I didn't want to tell you any of this. I didn't want to give you a reason to clam up around that man, not when he's someone who absolutely would appreciate you being yourself, being authentic. Don't put too much pressure on it, either. Just because I think the two of you would be great together, well...to be perfectly frank about it, what the hell do I know? It's not like I have a lot of young male friends, or even a lot of granddaughters, for that matter."

"So, what do you want me to do?" Jasmine's throat felt dry as the words squeaked out.

"Can you just be friends with him? I can text him and tell him to stop flirting with you—"

"Oh, I think I already put a stop to that," Jasmine interjected.

"All right, then." There was a hint of laughter in Viola's voice. "But friends...can you do that? It'll make it easier for the two of you to work together, and it'll probably make the time you spend together a lot more pleasant."

"And if we just *happen* to fall in love?" Jasmine knew the words had come out with a harsher bite than she had intended, but she was too raw to care.

"If that happens, I won't be mad about it," said Viola. "And I don't think you should be either. But don't put any pressure on yourself or on him. Just try to be cool. Can you be cool?"

Jasmine's laugh was humorless. "Have you met me, Grandma? Have I *ever* given you the impression of being cool?"

"All the time, dear. All the time. Of course, I'm still not entirely clear on what that word means."

Jasmine shook her head as she laughed. "That's a sick burn, Grandma, whether you meant it that way or not."

"Yes, well. If there's nothing else I can do for you, I should get back to Morty. He's giving me those puppy dog eyes and—"

"Got it, say no more." Jasmine held up a hand as if to create a physical barrier between herself and some words she *definitely* didn't need to hear. "Enjoy your trip, Grandma. See you when you're back. The cruise is bringing you back here in...what is it, two weeks?"

"Right, dear. We'll see you then." Viola's tone had changed. Jasmine raised an eyebrow, but she didn't press further. She would find out soon enough if there was something on her grandmother's mind.

Seven

Burak was waiting for her at the cat colony the following morning. She tried to pretend he wasn't, that it was a mere coincidence or similar schedules that had them there at the same time. But when he handed her a to-go cup of coffee and said, "I got this for you," she couldn't deny the truth any longer.

She smiled and thanked him. In truth, she had hoped to see him there that morning. He had been crossing her mind at increasing intervals since her conversation with her grandmother had ended, and though she had fallen asleep willing herself to think about absolutely anything else, he had popped right back into her mind as soon as she had woken up.

Cheddar was glad to see him, too, his small meows and the sound of claws on the hard plastic of the backpack compelling Jasmine to turn around so that the cat could see the object of his affection.

"Hi, Cheddar," Burak greeted him. "I can't take you out of there, bud. It wouldn't be safe, not here. You might get scared and run away and then your mom would be really upset with me. But I'll make it up to you another time. If that's alright with you, of course, Jasmine?" He raised his voice with his final words, and Jasmine turned to face him with a nod.

"Of course. I wanted to talk with you, too, about meeting Enes and Celia tonight. Does that work for you? We can reschedule if not, but I just thought you would want to get the project underway as soon as possible.

"No, that's perfect." Burak was nodding fervently. He gestured to the cats around them. "The sooner we get these guys settled, the better. I know it won't be an overnight thing. I mean, they're free agents and they'll probably find their way back here. But if we can get them sorted and settled somewhere safe, then by the time we're ready to break ground, hopefully there won't be any danger of them coming back and finding themselves in harm's way."

"Exactly." Jasmine took a sip of the coffee Burak had brought her, enjoying the heat of the comforting beverage in her throat on the cool morning. "I'll be the first to admit I don't know a thing about relocating a whole colony of cats. Though considering the expression 'like herding cats' exists, I'm guessing it won't exactly be a seamless transition."

"Right." Burak was looking at the base of a nearby wall, where a mother cat was eating some dry cat food, while her kittens played with her tail. "I believe it can be done, though. And I'm very hopeful that your friend will be able to help us."

Jasmine raised an eyebrow at him. "That's a lot of faith in someone you've never met and don't actually know anything about."

He looked back at her then and shrugged. "It's faith in your judgment, actually. If we're going to be partners in this business, then I think that's essential."

"So you didn't look Enes up online last night to see if he knew what he was talking about?" She crossed her arms over her chest, shifting her weight to one side.

Burak shook his head, his expression deadly serious. "Absolutely not. Of course, I don't know his last name, so it would have been pointless even if I had wanted to."

That got a small chuckle out of Jasmine before she checked the time on her phone. "I should head to the cafe. We were thinking of meeting at six o'clock tonight. Does that work for you? At a restaurant just down the road from the clinic."

"That sounds great. I'll pick you up at quarter to six then."

"Oh, no...you don't have to do that. I was going to go home first anyway and then just take a taxi." Jasmine waved him away with a hand. "It's fine. I can just meet you there."

Burak's eyes were sparkling as he smiled at her. "I'm afraid on this particular matter I can't take no for an answer. I can pick you up from your apartment if you prefer, or I can pick you up at the cafe, take you to your apartment, and wait for you in my car until you are ready to go. The choice is yours."

She knew her cheeks were heating, and she huffed in frustration. The last thing she wanted to do was explain to Burak that she had intended to change her clothes before they went out, because the last thing she needed was another clueless man giving her a once-over and telling her she looked just fine like she was. And if he was waiting in the car, he would definitely notice something like that.

"Fine," she said finally. "You can pick me up at my apartment."

"Wonderful," he replied with a nod before handing her his phone. "Now why don't you give me your phone number, so I can text you later to find out where exactly that is?"

Jasmine punched the keys with her fingers as she typed in the familiar number, an unfamiliar flicker of anticipation already blooming as she considered the evening ahead of her.

"Thanks," said Burak as he accepted his phone back from her, tapping a few buttons on the screen until Jasmine's phone began buzzing in her back pocket. She pulled it out, studying the unfamiliar number there. "Now you have my number, too."

"Or now you know for sure that I didn't give you a fake number," she quipped without thinking. "I mean...I don't know why I said that. It's not like you're a random dude in a bar that I'm trying to get rid of."

He raised an eyebrow. "Indeed I am not. I'm just your friendly neighborhood cat wrangling partner, and it would inconvenience both of us if you'd given me a fake number. I would have had to drive around the entire neighborhood and knock on way too many apartment doors before I found you."

She scoffed. "Yeah, right. Why bother with all that effort? You would have gone home, put your feet up, and put the whole thing out of your mind."

"Never." Burak shook his head. "You assume I would have reacted out of spite once I realized you had intentionally given me the wrong phone number. But that's the thing you apparently don't realize about me, Jasmine." Why did the way her name sounded on his lips make her feel things in her belly? Burak's expression was serious as his eyes bored into her. "I could never assume the worst of you. And the thought that you were at home, waiting for me and fearing that *you* had been stood up would keep me out in the streets, ringing bells and calling up to balconies until an annoyed neighbor threw a bottle at my head or called the police."

It was difficult to know what to say in response to that, so Jasmine merely nodded. "Got it," she said finally. "Glad you have the right number, then."

"Me, too. Even though I've always wanted to live out my own *Romeo and Juliet* balcony scene."

Jasmine felt her nose wrinkle. "I get the appeal of the dramatic, throwing pebbles at a window or a balcony, but maybe could you make a reference that doesn't end with two teenagers suffering the ultimate consequence all because no one knew how to communicate?"

Burak chuckled. "Fair enough. I'm out of here, anyway." He reached for her elbow, pulling her in lightly as his cheek brushed hers, first on the left and then on the right, the movement so automatic that he didn't even react, though she had gone stiff as soon as his body had approached hers. "See you tonight."

And with that, he was gone.

Jasmine was left standing there with the scent of his cologne—cedar and citrus—lingering faintly on her senses, the soft brush of stubble a phantom on her cheeks. She had been in Turkey long enough to know the gesture wasn't romantic, that cheek kisses didn't warrant the over-thinking she was tempted to give them.

But even knowing that didn't stop her from doing just that. And so, despite the lack of his physical presence, Burak lingered with her for the rest of the day.

Eight

"**C**ome *on*, Cheddar!" Jasmine was on her knees, pleading with the cat who had wedged himself under the couch in the front window of the cafe. She had already finished closing up for the evening, feeling good about being ahead of schedule and having enough time to freshen up and maybe even throw on some mascara before Burak arrived at her apartment to pick her up.

That was, of course, until Cheddar staged a silent protest, his eyes reflecting wide pupils back at her as she shined her cell phone's flashlight under the piece of furniture.

There was no good reason for him to be under the couch, nothing that Jasmine could wrap her mind around anyway. There hadn't been any loud noises or bigger cats coming down with a case of the zoomies and chasing him around.

No, everything had been business as usual while she had finished washing up and wiping down the tables. It was only when she had unzipped the cat backpack and crouched down on her knees that Cheddar had made a beeline for the furthest corner of the couch.

"Oh, duh. Of course." Jasmine smacked her forehead lightly with her open palm. Was this the worst possible moment for Cheddar to develop an aversion to the backpack? Or would any moment actually be inconvenient and annoying?

"This isn't going to work, buddy," she called under the couch, willing the cat to understand the full weight of her words. "The backpack is a necessary evil. The alternative is staying at the apartment all day, and we all know you don't want that." It went without saying that after his last stunt with the curtains, staying at the cafe overnight wasn't even an option.

She tried everything. With the enticement of a tasty treat, Cheddar edged closer to the front of the couch, but scooted back as soon as she moved the treat a few inches closer to herself. When she dangled his favorite toy, a paw darted out from under the couch, but disappeared just as quickly.

Jasmine checked the time, dismayed to see that she was going to be late. Burak was due to pick her up at her apartment in five minutes, and even if Cheddar leaped out from the couch and straight into her backpack, there was no way she would be there in time.

She texted him.

"I'm still at the cafe, trying to get Cheddar out from under the couch. Can you pick me up there instead?"

"And if you happen to be able to coax a kitten out of his hiding place, then that would be great, too," she muttered to herself as she got to her feet. She certainly hoped Burak would prove able to work a kitten-wrangling miracle, or else the future prospects of the curtains weren't looking good.

Just a few moments later, there was a gentle knock on the door and Jasmine hurried over to unlock it as Burak's eyes found hers when he leaned in, shielding his face with his hand to cut the glare.

"I heard there was an emergency?" he said with a smile, holding up a plastic bag.

She studied the bag for a second with a raised eyebrow before nodding at him. "Emergency might be a strong word, but there's definitely an unmanageable situation. I've never quite figured out how to get Cheddar to do something he doesn't want to do before, and I think he's finally clued in to what happens at this time of day, specifically that it's when he gets unceremoniously scooped into the cat backpack and has to make the bumpy journey home, and even though he really likes being at home, I don't exactly think he likes getting there—"

"Breathe, Jasmine." Burak's hands were on her upper arms, a thrill of electricity coursing between the two points of contact as he leaned down to look into her eyes. "I realize this seems like a very serious problem right now, but I promise it isn't fatal. Cheddar isn't *stuck* under the couch, right? Pinned underneath it somehow?"

Jasmine recoiled. "No, of course not."

"Right. Good." Burak nodded. "I figured if that were the case, you would have lifted the couch off him, like an adrenaline-fueled mother lifting a car to save a child. So the way I see it, as long as he isn't stuck, he's got to come out at some point. He'll get hungry or thirsty or bored or need to use the litter box."

Jasmine grimaced. "Right, but we don't have the time to wait it out." She checked the time again. "We're supposed to leave, well...*now* if we're going to meet Celia and Enes on time."

He raised one eyebrow at her. "And you don't think they would understand if you pushed our meeting back or even rescheduled it for a different day?"

"Of course they would." She gulped. "But we don't have the time for that, Burak. The colony...the more we delay this, the more of a last-minute disaster it's going to be. And I want to do this right."

He paused for a moment before dropping his hands and stepping away from her towards the couch. "You text your friends, or call them, whatever sort of communication you all like to use with each other...tell them to order drinks without us and we'll be there as soon as we can. Hopefully in no more than half an hour."

Jasmine turned her head to the side, studying him from a different angle. "And what are you going to do?"

"I..." He rubbed his palms together and crouched down in front of the couch. "...am going to work a miracle."

Jasmine shook her head at him, but managed to stop herself from rolling her eyes. His comment may have sounded cocky out of context, but for just this moment she was willing to suspend her disbelief and take a chance on the fact that, just maybe, Burak was about to bail her out. And if he didn't succeed, it's not as if she would be any worse off than she already was.

She fired off her message to Celia and then turned to find Burak crouched down in front of the couch, making soft noises to Cheddar. She couldn't make out what he was saying, so she simply stopped and observed.

"Er...what can I do?" she asked with hesitation.

He looked over his shoulder at her, giving her a smile and a small shake of his head. "You can put your feet up for a minute and take a break. We're just having a little man-to-man chat over here, but we'll figure it out. You don't need to worry about a thing."

"Are you sure? I could—" She was gesturing towards the back of the cafe, formulating some vague plan of finding something there to entice Cheddar out from his hiding place when Burak interrupted her thoughts.

"I'm sure," he said. He nodded towards the bag he had dropped on the floor next to himself. "I brought reinforcements."

With only thinly veiled curiosity, Jasmine took a seat where she could watch Burak unseen. She smiled at the gentle way he spoke to the cat, at his eagerness to help her out, to solve this problem for her, at every new treat and toy he pulled out of the bag.

And sure enough, it worked. It was only a few moments before Burak held Cheddar in his hands, and if the loud purrs emanating from the small beast were any indication, they were equally pleased about it. Burak was grinning, his chest puffed out in pride, and Jasmine rushed to her feet to approach them, holding out the backpack for Burak to deposit the cat inside.

"That's amazing. You really are a cat whisperer," she said. "That gives me a lot of hope for our colony relocation plan. Thank you so much." But as she held the backpack closer to Cheddar, he began to scramble, trying to get away. "Why does he hate this thing all of a sudden?" She lowered the backpack, her free hand coming up to her forehead. "I don't know what I'm going to do if this becomes a nightly occurrence."

"Hey." Burak's hands were both occupied with Cheddar, who was scrambling less but still not back to his previous relaxed state, so he reached with his elbow to nudge her upper arm. "We'll figure it out."

Jasmine scoffed before she could stop herself. "Sorry, but you being a cat whisperer doesn't exactly help me long-term, now does it? Unless you're saying you want to do this every evening." She gestured towards the cat, who was now cuddled against Burak's chest, once again purring.

Burak tilted his head down, looking at her through his lashes. "While that wasn't what I was offering, I'd gladly do it if the need arose." He looked down at the cat, scratching him behind his ear. "This little guy is growing on me, and I don't actually mind spending the time with you either."

She felt her cheeks heat at his words, but before she could object, he kept going.

"I just meant there has to be a solution. Maybe it's forming a positive connotation with the backpack for him. Have you tried that?"

Jasmine shook her head, a sudden awareness that she was the least qualified person in the room to run a cat cafe dawning on her. "I know it's important to get them used to new things, but...well, the first time I put him in the backpack, I just really needed to get home and get him there with me. I know it wasn't ideal, but I sort of figured that with time, he would get used to it."

Burak turned Cheddar over in his arms, stroking his belly as the cat stretched its paws up towards his face. Jasmine felt a pang in her chest at the cuteness of the moment, forcing her eyes to stay locked on Burak's so that she wouldn't say "Aww" out loud.

"Well, why don't we try something different today?" Burak tilted his head towards the bag he had brought with him. "Maybe a treat and a toy that he only gets when he's in the backpack...do you think that could work?"

"It already sounds better than just being unceremoniously shoved in there, doesn't it?" She was nodding as she spoke, for the first time letting herself feel hopeful that they might actually figure this particular dilemma out.

Five minutes later, Cheddar was in the backpack, curled on his side with a catnip mouse clasped in his front paws as he bunny kicked it with his back legs. Burak finished zipping the closure shut and then turned to face Jasmine.

"That wasn't so bad, was it?"

She shook her head. "It wasn't. And even though I'm thinking of all the ways it might not work in the future..." She trailed off, letting herself smile at him.

"It's enough to be glad that it worked tonight, isn't it?"

She nodded, feeling her smile spread wider. "It is. And I couldn't have done it without you." She surprised herself by reaching for his hand, her palm settling across the back of his knuckles. "Thank you. Really. You saved us both."

Burak gave her a grin that crinkled his eyes at the corner. "You are very welcome, though I fully believe you would have managed just fine without me. I'm still glad I could be here to share the experience." He picked up the backpack and nodded towards the door. "Now, shall we get this little fellow home to your apartment so we can get on with our evening?"

Jasmine reached for the backpack, but Burak shook his head, lifting it to his own shoulder as he nodded towards his car. As they left the cafe, locking the door behind her, she felt a faint flutter of butterflies at the awareness that Burak was accompanying to her home—well, to *Viola's* home, but it was still the place where she lived and slept and let her guard down. This hadn't been included in their original plan, of course. He was supposed to be downstairs waiting for her, and she was going to make a dramatic entrance, not at all unlike a scene from a teen movie, and there would be no need at all for him to come upstairs, to enter her space.

She was unusually quiet on the journey, speaking up only to tell Burak where to turn as her mind raced through different possibilities. Was there a way to keep him waiting in the car? Something to distract him with there? And if he did come upstairs, were her freshly laundered bras and underwear really laid out on the drying rack in her kitchen, or was that just the stuff of a bad dream?

She had almost settled on handing him her phone and telling him he simply *had* to try playing the latest matching game she had downloaded—though why sharing her unlocked cell phone with him unsupervised felt less invasive than letting him into her grandmother's apartment was a mystery of the highest order—when they arrived in the parking lot of her building.

"I can wait here," Burak offered, not meeting her eyes. "You can run up and drop off Cheddar, and I'm sure you don't need me for that."

Jasmine shook her head at herself, at what she was about to say. Why was it that the slight flush of his cheeks, the hesitation and vulnerability that suggested he would love to accompany her upstairs but didn't feel he had the right to ask...why was it that all of that made her want to let him in?

"Nonsense," she said as she unbuckled her seatbelt. "Who's going to play with Cheddar while I freshen up if you stay down here?" And with that she opened the door, slid out of the car, and started walking towards the door, knowing without even bothering to look that Burak was right behind her. She kept herself moving, kept the momentum pushing her forward so that she could avoid asking herself why she was suddenly willing to let down one layer of boundaries with this man, why the thought of having him in her home, sitting on her couch was suddenly something she desired rather than something that would make her shudder with dread.

They made it up the stairs of the old building in record time, and before Jasmine knew it, they were in front of the apartment door, unlocking the deadbolt as they both slipped off their shoes and Cheddar meowed in anticipation. "Oh right, I should probably warn you," said Jasmine over her shoulder as she made the final turn of the key. "There's another cat inside, and he's probably going to be nowhere near as happy to see you as Cheddar will be when we let him out. I just want to manage your expectations, so you don't take it personally when Gator sniffs you and then promptly hides himself under the bed."

Burak chuckled softly, and she was suddenly aware of just how close behind her he was as she felt the sound even more than she heard it. "I appreciate the warning," he said, touching the backpack that was slung over her shoulder. "How does Cheddar feel about Gator? Do they get along?"

"Oh, he's obsessed with him. Typical orange cat antics, as far as I understand. And he's completely unbothered by Gator's indifference. It works for now, at least, and I'm hopeful that by the time he's old enough to settle down a bit, they'll get along just great."

They were inside now, and Jasmine slipped the backpack to the ground to release Cheddar into the hallway of the apartment. Just as she had predicted, Gator poked his head into the hallway from the bedroom before disappearing back inside.

She gestured towards the living room, cringing at the sight of her drying rack full of intimate apparel. Rushing in ahead of Burak, she awkwardly folded the drying rack on itself, no small feat considering that it was still loaded down with socks and underwear. "Why don't you have a seat in here?" she offered, squeezing through the doorway with the metal contraption banging against the walls. "I'll just take this..."

Inside her bedroom, Jasmine closed the door behind her, leaning against it and letting her head drop into the wood. Gator was watching her from the bed with an appraising eye, and she shook her head at him. "Don't even start with me. You're the one hanging out in here when you *could* be out there sniffing a handsome stranger and having the time of your life."

Jasmine took a quick moment to change into a dress—the adventure of the couch had definitely made her work up a sweat—and throw her hair in a clip. She opened a tube of red lipstick, about to swipe it across her lips when she hesitated. "Is this too much?" she asked Gator. "Is he going to think I'm trying to impress him?"

Gator stretched and rolled onto his other side, the picture of unbothered feline bliss.

"Good point," said Jasmine with a nod. "We *are* going out on the town after all. And meeting friends, too. Lipstick it is."

When she emerged from the bedroom a few moments later, Gator was at her heels, as if he had heeded her words and really did want to meet Burak—or as if he wanted to be entertained by whatever reaction her makeover drummed up.

Jasmine wasn't sure what she had expected to find in the living room, but judging by Cheddar's typical energy level after a day at the cafe, there wasn't much that would have surprised her. Hanging from a light fixture? That wasn't out of the realm of possibility. Tap dancing across lit flames on the gas stove? It hadn't happened before, but that didn't mean it wouldn't happen one day.

The only thing she definitely *hadn't* expected to find was Cheddar snuggled into the crook of Burak's arm, sound asleep with his fuzzy belly exposed. Even more surprising than that, Burak was petting said belly...and there was no blood dripping from his hand at all, no indication of any kind that Cheddar had attacked him for daring to touch his soft fur.

"Huh." The words came out before Jasmine could stop them, and Burak's head turned with a jerk to look at her over his shoulder.

"Hi," he said. His smile was sheepish, morphing into something unrecognizable as his eyes scanned her, taking in her transformation of the previous moments. He swallowed, blinking slowly. "You look nice," he said, at last, before glancing down at himself. "Now I'm wondering if I'm too casual to be seen next to you."

"Nonsense," said Jasmine with a wave of her hand, once again looking for some surface she could busy herself with tidying rather than coming closer to Burak. She found the mug from her early morning coffee in the sink and set to washing it, glancing over her shoulder at Burak. "Besides, orange cat hair really elevates any outfit."

He grimaced. "Right, didn't think about that." He was looking down at the kitten with such a soft smile that Jasmine had to look away. "It wasn't as if I could say no to him, though. He might actually be the cutest cat I've ever met, but don't tell anyone I said that."

When the mug was rinsed and placed in the drying rack, Jasmine wiped her hands on a dish towel before taking a few tentative steps towards Burak. "Your secret's safe with me, but I'm not entirely sure who you're keeping it from. Is it that you don't want anyone to know that you're a softie who loves cats? Because if they see you feeding the strays, the jig will definitely be up."

Burak slid Cheddar from his lap, repositioning him on the couch cushion so seamlessly that his eyes only blinked open for a slow second before he settled back into his sleep. "No." Burak's voice was quieter as he got up, easing himself away from Cheddar. "I don't want him to know. Don't want it to go to his head." He shrugged. "And it's probably for the best if the other cats don't know either. Don't want the secret that I have a favorite to get out."

Gator took that moment to issue a plaintive meow, and Burak bit his lower lip with chagrin.

"Hey buddy. Didn't see you there," he said, dropping to a knee to hold out a hand for Gator to sniff. "Isn't this Ms. Viola's cat?"

Jasmine nodded. "He is, but he stayed behind. Something about pets not being allowed on the cruise ship."

Burak looked around the room as he got back to his feet. "Won't you miss all of this when she comes back? What are you going to do then?" His eyes widened as soon as the question was out, as if he had surprised himself by asking about it. "Sorry, that's none of my business."

"No, it's okay." She gestured towards the door. "We can head out, and I'll answer your question on the way. That'll give me a minute to think about what my answer is."

He narrowed his eyes slightly, but started to move towards the door. "You really haven't thought about it? Doesn't that stress you out?"

Jasmine sighed. "It's not that, not really. I was so aimless before I came here, that I've really just been enjoying the steady routine. The regular rhythm of opening the cafe, knowing what each day holds. Even having the time to paint again a little bit."

"You paint?" They had made it to the door by then, but Burak paused with his hand on the knob, looking around as if evidence of Jasmine's painting was hiding somewhere he could see if he just craned his neck a little more.

She nodded, placing a hand on his shoulder to urge him forward and feeling a twinge of surprise or electricity at the contact. "I do, but that's a story for another time."

"You'll show me your work the next time I come over?"

Through gritted teeth, she answered. "Fine."

She could hear the smile in Burak's voice. "Then it's a date."

Nine

When they finally connected with Celia and Enes at their favorite bar, Jasmine was a confused mess of emotions, wanting nothing more than to pull her friend into the bathroom for some much needed girl talk.

It wasn't just that Burak had saved the day where Cheddar was concerned. Or how sweetly the large man and tiny cat had been, snuggled up on her couch waiting for her. It was also an unspoken something that they shared, a way that they moved together that could almost trick her into thinking they were a couple. The way he had held open doors for her, first the apartment's door and then the passenger door of the car. The way he had moved to the street side of the sidewalk every time they had been walking side by side. The way he leaned in to speak to her, coming so close she could feel his voice more than hear it. The fingertips that found her lower back, guiding her around a group of tourists.

And even though Jasmine knew it would be bad manners to pull Celia aside as soon as the introductions were made, she poured every bit of faith she had in the power of female friendship into her friend getting an accurate read on the situation and setting aside some time as soon as possible so that the two of them could do a full postmortem of this evening and everything that had preceded it.

It was easy to find the table where her friends were waiting, the safe haven of their familiar presence calling to Jasmine's unsettled nervous system like a beacon summoning a ship lost at sea. She picked up the pace to get to them, reluctantly dropping away from Burak's palm on her lower back and hurrying to the safety of her friend's side.

"Burak, this is Celia and Enes. Celia, Enes...this is Burak." She hurried to sit down across from Celia as they all shook hands and exchanged greetings, working to school her expression into something resembling cool and collected, but failing, judging by the way Celia's eyebrows climbed as their eyes met.

"Good to see you guys," said Enes, stretching his arm behind Celia, who leaned back into his touch. "And of course to meet you, Burak. I hear we have a cat colony issue to work out together."

Celia threw her head back as she laughed. "My fiance, ladies and gentlemen. Skips the niceties and gets right down to business!" She turned to Enes and smiled. "At least where cats are concerned. And considering that it was our love of cats that brought us together, I suppose I can't fault you for it."

"Right." Enes's cheeks were pink. "Should we at least order you two some drinks before we get down to business?"

Burak was nodding, but Jasmine was shaking her head, her hands gesturing for Enes to stop talking. "Hold on just a minute there." She leaned forward. "Did you say *fiance*?"

Celia's eyes were twinkling as she nodded, reaching across the table to show off a sparkly engagement ring.

"We're just engaged by American standards, of course," said Enes. "We haven't done the ceremony with my relatives yet, or anything, so..."

"If I happen to run into any of your aunts, don't say anything? No problem!" But Jasmine was smiling at both of them as she studied Celia's ring, her eyes darting between the two as she tried to figure out which one of them thought they were the lucky one in this pairing. "I'm really happy for you both."

"As am I," Burak piped up. "Of course, I didn't know you before you were engaged, but it still feels like this calls for a celebration. What are you drinking? Is this a champagne toast sort of occasion?"

Celia shook her head, gesturing to her nearly empty wine glass. "Red wine. And snacks. The celebration of champions!" She turned to Enes, pursing her lips. "We should get a bottle, right? To share? And these two should plan to drink too much and then take a taxi home, right?" She turned back to face Jasmine and Burak, already nodding. "You can't let us celebrate alone, you know." But then she leaned forward and whispered loudly. "Of course you can say no if you really want to. Peer pressure sucks. I'm just saying, though, if you want a good excuse to have a little too much fun and don't want to feel irresponsible taking a taxi home when you *could* have just stuck to water and then driven yourself home—"

Burak held up a finger, as if waiting his turn to speak, and Celia cut herself off. "I like the way you think. And I actually have a meeting in this part of the city tomorrow morning, so if I leave my car here, it's no problem at all." He leaned back and looked around for a waiter, gesturing with a smile when he made eye contact with one. "Let's get this party started! Which wine was it?"

"The pinot noir," said Celia to him, before repeating it again to the waiter. "And two more glasses, please."

"And we'll take two orders of fries," Enes chimed in, before glancing around the table. "Anything else?"

"How about some hummus?" asked Jasmine. The gathering had quickly taken on the feeling of four old friends embarking on a night to remember and she couldn't think of the last time she'd felt this excited to be out. Or, actually, the last time she'd been out of her apartment this late in the evening. Certainly the last time she'd been sitting mere inches away from a handsome and attentive man.

Speaking of which...

Jasmine chanced a glance at Burak, only to find his eyes were already on her. Her cheeks immediately began to heat, the feeling that she had been caught looking at him filling her with embarrassment, all logical thoughts that he had, in fact, been looking at her *first* evaporating before they had a chance to form.

Though she had turned her attention away from him as soon as their eyes had met, she felt rather than saw him lean towards her, his mouth coming close to her ear.

"I like your friends," he said. "And I'm glad we're doing this. It's nice to spend time with you outside of the cafe."

"Almost like we're friends?" she asked, her eyes darting to his, down to his mouth that was now dangerously close to her cheek, and then back up to his eyes.

His pupils widened almost imperceptibly. "Something like that." He leaned in closer. "I'd settle for being your friend, but just know that it's not my first choice."

Oh, here we go again, thought Jasmine, shaking her head slightly as she leaned away from Burak and back towards the table where their glasses were now being delivered. As she slid Burak's glass over to him, she chanced another glance in his direction, expecting to see him looking pleased with himself for yet again making her blush with his exaggerated flirtation. She was already preparing for her next conversation with her grandmother, where she would turn her chiding of the older woman up another level. Her grandma could call Burak and tell him the plan was off, that her matchmaking skills had been entirely off base, and that he needed to cool it.

But what she saw on his face surprised her. He was smiling, but he didn't look smug. If anything, the smile didn't quite reach his eyes and had the slightest downturn at the corners. When he noticed her looking, he gave her the slightest of nods and an almost-wink, mouthing something that looked like, "It's okay, don't worry about it."

What the—?

Was he genuinely interested in her? What had seemed to be just a bit of fun now had all the makings of something serious. Something with the potential for feelings to get hurt and relationships—especially business relationships—to get complicated.

Jasmine only realized she was lost in her thoughts when Celia appeared at her elbow, bodily hauling her to her feet. "Come on," said her friend, "I need to visit the ladies' room, and you know the rule. If one of us goes, both of us go." She looked back at the men. "You guys can bond while we're gone. If you wanted to figure out the whole cat problem of yours so we can move on to other subjects when we return, I wouldn't mind at all."

Jasmine let herself be dragged along by her friend, only removing her arm from Celia's grasp when they were inside the restroom, standing in front of the sinks.

"What's going on with you and Burak?" Celia asked, hands finding her hips. "And don't tell me there's nothing there and pretend you don't know what I'm talking about. I see all the looks shot between the two of you, the way he looks at you when he thinks you aren't looking...there's chemistry there, and I'm just trying to figure out why you're hiding it from me. Are you guys dating?" She pulled a face. "Is it...a hookup? I don't know what you kids are calling things these days."

Now it was Jasmine's turn to plant her hands on her hips. "Don't act like you're older than me just because you're engaged, Celia. And no, to answer your question, we aren't dating or hooking up or whatever you want to call it. I'm not hiding anything from you, and I *genuinely* don't know what you're talking about."

Celia let out a tiny gasp. "You really don't, do you?" She reached to pull Jasmine into a one-sided embrace, Jasmine stubbornly refusing to wrap her arms around her friend. "Oh, you poor sweet summer child," continued Celia, aggressively rubbing her hand up and down Jasmine's back.

"That man *really* likes you. And even if you don't want to admit it to yourself, I think there's a pretty good chance you like him, too."

Jasmine pulled back enough to look at her friend's face, but Celia's grip was tight and she wasn't able to wrest herself free. "What do you mean? What are you talking about? Is this the jet lag talking or did you...I don't know...accidentally drink a bottle of nail polish remover?" She forced a hand between them, holding up three fingers in front of Celia's eyes. "How many fingers am I holding up?"

Celia pushed her hand away with a small laugh and stepped back, finally releasing Jasmine from her grip. "It's cute how oblivious you are. But you and that man need to have a talk, Jas. If you don't lay your cards out on the table, then whatever this *thing* between you is, it's likely to build up so much pressure that it explodes in your face. And I'm not saying that you should date him or make him your boyfriend or anything like that...I just think you both need to be honest about what you want and see if you're on the same page." She lifted her hands in a shrug. "Maybe I'm reading everything totally wrong and he's crazy about you and you are utterly indifferent about him. In that case, let him down easy."

Jasmine swallowed. "But you don't think that's the case, do you?"

Celia shook her head. "I definitely do not. If the way you are with him is how you behave with someone you feel indifferent about, then I guess I've only ever seen you around people who are your mortal enemies. And I'm trying not to be offended that apparently I fall into that category, too."

A deep sigh escaped from Jasmine's lips before she could stop it. "We did talk about this, actually. Burak and I did. I mean, we didn't talk about both of us being interested in each other because I'm still in complete denial of that particular statement." She rubbed her temples, feeling overcome with the exhaustion of the day. "We talked about how he was flirting with me and how my grandmother was basically trying to match make the two of us."

Celia's smile was so infuriating that Jasmine had to bite the inside of her cheek to stop herself from saying something she would regret. Instead, she merely raised an eyebrow and gave the smallest shake of her head, an unspoken yet clearly communicated, "What?"

"I have a feeling I would really like your grandma. And I also have a feeling that maybe you shouldn't be so quick to dismiss her intuition about this particular subject, this particular match."

"It's not like she's ever even seen me and Burak together! How could she possibly know if there's chemistry between us?" Jasmine demanded. "Am I the only one who has learned this lesson from Hollywood and movies and all the behind-the-scenes podcasts? Just because two people are attractive or just because they are both talented actors, that *doesn't* mean there will be chemistry between them! That's why they have screen tests and chemistry reads and why sometimes movies with the best casts still flop."

Celia was looking at her like she had two heads. "You realize you're talking about *movies*, right? Acting? Fiction? A setting in which there are a myriad of actors to choose from for both leading roles and where you need a unique skill set in order to even image all the possible combinations and permutations? Where people can win awards for casting because it is truly an art and a science?"

Through gritted teeth, Jasmine spoke. "Yes. Your point?"

"How many grandchildren does Viola have? Just you?" When Jasmine nodded, Celia bobbed her head along with her. "And so you'd say she knows you pretty well, yeah?" Another nod. "Is it possible then that this is, in fact, *not* a situation where your grandmother is randomly assigning two actors to a scene and then wondering if they will gel but is *actually* the sort of scenario where, knowing and loving *you*, her granddaughter, as much as she does, having you always on her mind and in her heart, she met a young man and felt a deeper intuitive nudge that there might be *something* there?"

"It's possible." It was physically painful to force the words out. "I'm not saying it's likely or probable," she hurried to add, "but I am not stubborn enough to say that it's physically impossible."

"Good." Celia smiled. "That's a start, then. At least you're open to it." She nodded towards the door. "Come on, then. Let's get back to the table. Our dates are waiting."

Ten

"I really liked your friends," said Burak, turning his head to face her in the back of the taxi. True to Enes's suggestion, they had stayed out longer than intended and the wine had flowed slightly more freely than Jasmine had planned. She was warm and relaxed as she reflected on the evening they had shared.

"They liked you, too." She put her hand on top of Burak's and gave a soft squeeze before catching herself and sliding it back to her lap and looking out the window again. "And I think we've got a solid plan for the colony now. It feels a little silly, doesn't it? Like, we probably could have just looked it up online and watched a video. We didn't have to rope in a whole veteran...veterin...veterinarian." She giggled as she stumbled over the word. "We should get started soon. Tomorrow, maybe."

When she glanced over, Burak's shoulders were up in an exaggerated shrug, his inhibitions at least as relaxed as her own. "I can forgive us for that," he said. "It was too important to just leave it to Google, you know? It's...I mean, it's their *family*, Jas. We can't mess that up. Separate the cats from their families, break up their bonds..." He shook his head, and she could see from the curve of his brow that he was deadly serious. "I would feel like such a monster if we did that. You would, too."

"I would?" She tried to ignore the way his shortening of her name, the affection and intimacy of it felt, flicking around in her lower belly.

Burak nodded. "We aren't so different, you and me. I mean, we aren't the same, either. Case in point, I like you more than you like me. But we both like cats." He tipped his head back and forth as if weighing his next words. "You might be a little more overt about it, what with the whole cat cafe thing. And I might pretend I'm not as big a fan of them as you are, but we both know that's not really the truth."

Jasmine picked the safest statement of his to respond to. "You never had me fooled. From the first time I saw you, you were feeding a whole flock of cats and then it only got more obvious from there."

The taxi pulled up in front of her building, and before she could wish Burak a good night, she saw that he was already opening his door as well. *Ever the gentleman*, she thought, realizing that he was going to insist on seeing her safely to her door, perhaps going on to walk home from her apartment, now that his car was tucked in for the night on the other side of town.

As they walked towards the door together, the words burst out of her. "You like me more than I like you?"

Burak nodded. "Obviously."

She stopped and turned to face him. "No. You just like to flirt, and maybe my grandmother got into your head about some potential sparks between us." She shook her head. "That doesn't mean you like me. Maybe you're just bored. You need a hobby. Or an actual crush, because then you'll realize that *isn't* what this is. You know what I mean?"

Burak only shook his head, his expression as serious as she had ever seen it. "I'm afraid that not even you can tell me what I feel, Jas." He gestured towards himself. "I contain multitudes. Depth of feeling you can't even imagine contained in this body of mine."

A shiver teased its way up Jasmine's spine, and she clamped her lips together to stop herself from dismissing Burak and his words, playing off the way they had impacted her. "Okay," she said finally, her voice small.

"Okay?" he asked, cocking his head slightly to the side. "Is that you giving me permission to like you, or...?"

Jasmine sighed. "I don't know what it is. Me accepting that there's a chance that could be true, I suppose. Not trying to talk you out of it."

"Entertaining the possibility?"

She gave him a small nod, which caused a smile to spread across his lips.

"So, will you let me take you out tomorrow? I mean, on a date, just to be clear."

"A date where we relocate a colony of cats?"

Burak shook his head. "No. After that. A date where the two of us go out and have fun together and we don't pretend we aren't interested in something more."

"I wasn't—" She let her sentence drop off at a look from him that seemed to go right through the outer layers of her persona. "Maybe I was," she admitted with a sigh.

"Maybe I have been in denial this whole time just because I don't want my grandmother to be right. Just because I'm stubborn."

"That's one of my favorite things about you." He held up a hand. "And before you can say that I don't know you well enough to have favorite things about you, please keep in mind that I was hearing about you daily for six months. Every time I crossed paths with your grandmother at the bakery, in fact. I had plenty of time to come up with a list of theoretical things I might simply adore about you, and it only took a few moments to confirm that my intuition on that matter had been, frankly, exceptional."

There wasn't much Jasmine could think of to say in response to Burak's proclamation. She nodded at him, grateful for the relative darkness that was covering the flush of her cheeks. They continued the remaining steps to her apartment, and as she pushed the front door open, he leaned in. He pulled her body to his for the quickest of embraces, murmuring, "See you tomorrow then," as his lips grazed her temple.

"See you tomorrow," she replied, turning to face him and seeing only his retreating back. She pulled her jacket closer against the chill in the air and jogged up the stairs, ready to be alone with her cats and process the evening that had left her feeling uncertain about so many things.

Eleven

By the time Jasmine was settled against her headboard with a mug of herbal tea and a purring cat on either side of her, her dress traded in for an old t-shirt and her softest sweatpants, the evening felt like a dream. She had thought she had known Burak and the space he occupied in her life well enough to have a handle on him, but when they had been out of their normal environment—and when their tongues had been loosened by wine and laughter—she was seeing him in a different light. And she couldn't stop staring at him in her mind, as if by doing so she could make sense of this new, unfamiliar person he had turned out to be.

"We're going to get your old colony settled tomorrow," she told Cheddar, who looked up at her with sleepy eyes, blinking as if he were trying to understand her words. "It turns out it's not that hard. We just have to move them all at once and keep them sort of enclosed in the new location, so they don't just head right back to their old home. I'm thinking the courtyard behind the cafe will be the perfect new home. Here I was thinking it was going to be a months-long process, like we'd have to move one cat per day or something. But by the sounds of it, it's pretty straightforward. Who knew?" Cheddar gave her another slow blink, and she nodded back at him. "Right," she said. "You knew. I should have asked you."

She scratched Cheddar behind the ear, replacing her mug on the bedside table so that she could reach for Gator with the other hand. "What am I doing here?" she wondered out loud, remembering Burak's questions when he had entered the apartment. "This...this feels like my life." She shook her head. "But it isn't. Grandma will be back soon, and she and Morty are going to want their space and then...well, Cheddar, you and I are going to be on our own." Her stomach dropped as a thought occurred to her. "Or *I* am going to be on my own, at least. Grandma will keep you in a second. And I know she would keep me too, but it doesn't really work that way for humans." She gave the sleepy kitten a sad smile. "I sort of have to figure things out on my own. Absurd, isn't it?"

Jasmine reached for her tea, taking a long sip as both cats curled deeper into themselves. "And what about Burak?" she asked herself. "I barely even want to let myself think about that whole thing. Does it make sense to go out with him? What's the point of even liking each other as more than friends, childish as that sounds? It's not like we're going to move in together and I'll stay in Istanbul forever. I'm going to be out of here soon, and we'll both probably just regret that we invested any emotional energy in each other." It didn't matter if that thought made her feel a twinge of sadness; it was the truth. "I'll go out with him tomorrow—it would be rude to cancel this late in the game, anyway—but that's going to be it. No more. I don't want his feelings to be hurt when it turns out that I can't give him what he wants." And okay, maybe she didn't want *her* feelings to be hurt, either. She wasn't a masochist, after all.

She switched off the bedside lamp and settled into the darkness, tossing and turning until both cats abandoned her to sleep elsewhere in the apartment. But no matter how much she flipped from side to side, sleep didn't come for her, and the hours until morning stretched ahead of her like the stretchiest string of gooey melted cheese.

Twelve

The new day dawned with exhaustion, under-eye shadows, and a strengthened resolve to refocus, to let Burak down gently. It would be a nice day, one Jasmine would remember for years to come, warmed with pride at how they had managed the relocation of the cats. She might even look back on it as a turning point in her own life, a time when she had rediscovered a commitment to herself and her life of (solo) adventure.

Soon, after all, it would be time to purchase a new sketch book, to trade in her canvases for a travel paint set, and a book full of blank pages small enough to tuck away into her backpack.

"Maybe I'll even trade my regular backpack in for that cat backpack," she said to Cheddar, who was twining around her legs as she applied her mascara. "What do you think, bud? Do you want to be a world traveler kitty, or do you want to make your case to Grandma to let you stay on here?"

It was impossible to decipher Cheddar's meows one way or the other, so Jasmine only smiled at him. "I'm sure we'll figure it out soon. She said she wanted to talk to me about something, and I don't think it would take any particular psychic gifts to figure out what it is."

Reaching up to dab a little color on the apples of her cheeks, Jasmine forced a smile to position the blush in just the right place. The gesture felt foreign, so out of alignment with her true feelings. It didn't make any sense that she should feel so down-hearted about leaving Istanbul, about giving the keys to the apartment back to her grandmother. It had been a nice, soft place to land when she needed it, but that certainly didn't mean she needed to mourn the end of this particular season.

She was supposed to be excited about the next season, the next adventure, dang it, so why wasn't she?

She looked down to find Cheddar sitting back on his haunches, blinking up at her expectantly.

"Is this your fault?" she asked him, the question kick-starting his purring so loud she was sure her neighbors would hear. She bent down to pet him, willing herself yet again to put her concerns for the future out of her mind. The day had enough in store already, without fears of the uncertainties she hadn't even imagined yet overtaking her awareness.

When Jasmine arrived at the colony half an hour later, her eyebrows climbed at the awareness that Burak and Enes had beaten her there. By the looks of it, the two men had been up for hours, considering that Burak had already traveled across the city to retrieve his car—and pick up Enes, too, which Jasmine couldn't remember arranging the night before.

"There she is!" Burak greeted her with a kiss on the cheek, pulling her closer with one hand on her elbow, before slipping a to-go cup of coffee into her hand. "Good morning." His smile communicated all of his excitement and hope for the day ahead, and she knew it was as much about the date they had arranged for the evening as the found family of cats currently eating their breakfast.

"Good morning, Burak," she said with a smile that conveyed only a fraction of what he had given her. Better to start rebuilding her walls now so that the conversation that needed to happen in the evening wouldn't be too much of a shock to the system. "And good morning to you too, Enes. Nice to see you here."

Enes smiled back before his attention was taken once again by the cats. Jasmine and Burak drank their beverages in companionable silence as they watched him make his way around the colony, assessing the situation.

Finally, he walked towards them with a nod. "Right," he began. "So here's the situation. It looks like you've got a group full of female cats and their litters of kittens. Some of the females are already neutered, and some aren't. They all seem companionable, no truly feral cats here, and the kittens are mostly of the age where they're just about weaned and ready to be on their own."

"So it's a community of strong women raising their children together?" Jasmine asked. "I love that."

Enes nodded. "That's often the dynamic of colonies, since male cats are more territorial."

"Well, I assume the kittens aren't all females, are they?" Burak asked. "What happens to the little boys, then?"

"They stay with the colony for a while, but you're right. It's not sustainable." Enes pursed his lips. "I think our best bet is to relocate the mothers with their kittens, and then to see about adoption options for the kittens. Maybe an event at the cafe, Jasmine. How would that sound to you?"

She was already nodding before the words were even out. "I would love that. It could be a whole event. Maybe a paint and sip evening, but with coffee and tea instead of wine? Or we could do, I don't know...a cat yoga class? A fundraiser for an animal shelter?" Her mind was buzzing with ideas, too many at once for her to even nail one down. The energy was vibrating through her, and she wished for nothing more than a blank page and a nice smooth pen to capture every single idea that was currently threatening to slip away into the ether if she didn't immortalize it on a piece of paper.

"All good ideas," said Enes. "And I'm more than happy to help with any veterinary needs. Sterilizations and immunizations and all of that. The most important thing will be getting these cats settled and safe in their new environment so that they don't end up wandering back here. It'll be a construction zone soon, and nobody wants to see anything tragic happen when tiny animals and heavy machinery attempt to coexist."

Burak's nod was deadly serious. "Absolutely not. We will get the cats to the new place, the courtyard. And then we will break ground as soon as possible. Changing the scenery drastically should help them realize it's no longer their home, right?"

Enes nodded, but there was some hesitation in the gesture. "That will partially help, but territorialism runs deeper than that. You'll still need to be careful."

"Got it," said Burak. "If I need to have one of my guys serving as a guard at the construction site, and another one escorting the cats back to their new home, then so be it."

Jasmine realized a beat too late that Burak's expression was serious, that he wasn't joking about putting his employees on "cat guard duty," and she felt herself warm to him even more. How on earth was she going to let him down easily? How was she supposed to feel good about denying herself the chance to be in his life, to have him in hers?

But that was a question for later. Enes was still relaying instructions for the great cat migration, expressing his regret that he couldn't be there that day, and she needed to glean any last-minute wisdom that she could.

It was decided then, once she and Burak were left to their own devices, that she would do one final check of the courtyard, while he began arranging the cat carriers and treats to lure the mama cats in advance.

"Good luck," he said, once more pressing a soft kiss to her cheek.

"You too," she replied. "See you soon."

Thirteen

I n the end, the day went off without a hitch. Whether it was because of his charm or because of his superior ability to pick the tastiest cat treats, by the time Jasmine returned to the abandoned lot to check on Burak's progress, all the cages were full, one mama cat and her kittens nestled inside each one, and the remaining cats were milling about.

"Well done," she said, unable to keep the surprise from her voice.

"You didn't think I could do it?" Burak's eyes were twinkling, but there was a note of challenge there in his voice.

"It wasn't anything to do with a lack of faith in *you*," she said. "More that herding cats is a notoriously impossible task."

"Well, since you weren't here to see how I got it done, then I suppose you'll just have to remain in awe of my powers." He winked at her then. "If I go revealing my secrets, then what need will you have to keep me around?"

Her smile was pained. She wished she *could* keep him around, but the problem was, of course, that she didn't even know where "around" was, where she would be in a month.

"Shall we, then?" She picked up the two cages that were closest to her, her concerns drowned out immediately by the plaintive meows of the cats inside.

A few of Burak's colleagues appeared then, and with all of them put to work, the cages were accounted for, and they began the short walk to Kedi Cafe. Jasmine wished for just a moment that there was someone there to document their procession, this parade of complaining cats walking a few short blocks, the saddest celebration a street like theirs had ever seen. Glancing over her shoulder, she was pleased to see that they were being followed, in fact, by the cats that hadn't deigned to enter one of the cages. The vacant lot was now truly vacant, and the entirety of the colony was on the move.

It was *working*.

The next test was the courtyard. When the cage doors were opened, would the cats make a break for it, or would they explore their new surroundings, settle in to their new home?

Burak had already been hard at work that morning. The courtyard was now equipped with beds and cat trees, a multilevel cat house for its new residents to sleep outside of the elements. One of Burak's colleagues had even carried a few of the ratty old beds the cats had been sleeping on in the vacant lot, in the hopes of the familiar smells speeding along the adaptation process.

The cages were placed on the ground as Jasmine and Burak distributed food and water, Burak's workers blocking the courtyard entrance once all the cats were inside.

She opened the door of the first cage, pleasantly surprised when the cat inside emerged, walked over to the freshly dispersed food and began to eat. Just like that. With no drama whatsoever. Whatever Jasmine had been anticipating, fearing...it wasn't happening.

As they continued to open cage doors, the responses of the cats and kittens inside were similarly anticlimactic.

Burak placed an arm around Jasmine's shoulders and pulled her in for a quick squeeze. "We did it," he said in a low voice. "We really did it."

"We did," she agreed, still shocked by how easy it had all been. It was just the beginning, of course. They would need to keep an eye on the cats and make sure they didn't return to the vacant lot—though by the looks of the calico and tabby cats who were settling in, one in a sunny spot next to the wall and one staking a claim on some prime real estate in the cat condo, there wasn't much to worry about on that front.

They would also need to keep moving forward with the kitten adoption, the fundraising, the veterinary care...Jasmine could feel her pulse picking up as she imagined attempting to cross everything off her list before her grandmother returned and the cafe was once again in her hands. It would be unfair of her to leave this project half finished for her grandma, and she would always wonder how it had all turned out if she didn't see it through to the end herself.

But that was a concern for tomorrow. For today, at least, she could celebrate the victory they had just seen.

And she could let Burak down easily, she thought, her mouth twisting at the reminder.

Take the good with the bad, she told herself. *You can still have a nice evening, even if it's the last one you get to spend together. No need to ruin it before it has even begun, is there?*

"I should get the cafe open," she said, checking the time on her phone. "Why don't you and your guys stop in for some drinks on the house before you head out?"

"That's very kind of you. Thanks."

Fourteen

Jasmine couldn't resist escaping to the courtyard in the slow moments at the cafe to check on the cats there. She knew—how could she not, after all the warnings her grandmother had given her when she had handed over the keys—better than to leave the cafe unattended and unlocked.

"The cats will know they're alone, and they'll get into all sorts of trouble," Viola had warned. "I learned that lesson the hard way myself, and I won't even tell you the extent of the horrors that were awaiting me in the kitchen." She shuddered. "Learn from my mistakes, Jasmine."

And so Jasmine had interpreted that warning to mean that, as long as a regular customer was settled in with a nice cup of coffee and the cafe and its cats weren't truly *unattended*, then there was no problem at all with ducking out for just a few moments.

She had done just that three times now, always feeling a wave of nerves travel her spine just as she was about to cross the threshold, a fear that the courtyard would be empty or some tragedy would be awaiting her. And every time she had felt warmed from within at the sight of peaceful cats bathing in the sun, kittens purring as she greeted them, the whole thing the picture of domestic feline bliss.

"I think we really did it," she said to herself with a nod, before returning to the cafe. "Not a fluke, but an actual success." The thought made her smile. She might be about to leave, might be just a few weeks away from never seeing the cats in the courtyard again, except for the occasional visit of course, but she could take pride in knowing she had done this one thing right.

She had taken a picture of the courtyard in all its glory, and she sent it along with a short text message to her grandmother then.

"Look at this. Forgot to tell you before, but this was a project Burak and I were working on, relocating the cats from a construction site. I think they like their new home!"

Jasmine expected her grandmother's eventual response to be nothing more than some heart eyed emojis or maybe a whole line of thumbs ups—Grandma was *really* into emojis these days—but she didn't expect it anytime soon.

So she was surprised when her phone vibrated in her hand with a new message.

"Amazing! They look so happy. Can we talk tonight? Got some things I need to run by you xx"

Jasmine forced down the anxious pang in her stomach. She had known this was coming, of course, but it still didn't mean she was immune to worrying about all the potential bad news her favorite person might be prepared to drop on her.

As if in answer to her feelings, her phone buzzed with one more message from her grandmother.

"It's nothing bad, everyone is healthy, and you aren't in trouble. I think it's actually a GOOD thing that I want to share with you xx"

Her smile was broad then, as she texted her response. Of course it was a good thing for her grandma to be coming home, and she was relieved that there was nothing else that was about to be sprung on her.

"Can't wait. I'm going out with Burak tonight—don't get excited, nothing is happening there—but I should be home by...10? Talk to you then?"

Jasmine laughed out loud at the response that came almost immediately. Whoever had taught her grandma how to use the "eyes" emoji to suggest she was detecting something fishy deserved a raise. Okay, it was Jasmine herself who had conveyed that lesson, and of course she knew *she* deserved a raise.

"Don't cut things early on my account. And now I have to add something else to the agenda for our conversation: Burak!"

Jasmine's smile faded at that. She would have something to report about Burak by the time she spoke to Grandma, and she had a strong feeling that neither of them were going to like it.

Fifteen

Burak picked her up at her apartment that evening, texting to let her know he had arrived downstairs but to take her time. For just a moment, she considered inviting him upstairs to greet the cats, who she knew would be thrilled at his presence, but she thought better of it before her fingers even touched the keypad on her phone. The more she could do to begin extricating Burak from her life, the smoother the inevitable transition would be when she left.

Instead, she sent him a "Be right down!" and threw her hair into a ponytail, taking one last look at herself in the mirror. She had made an effort—another dress pulled from the back of her closet, another red lipstick—but not so much of one that Burak would be haunted by her stunning beauty, forever remembering her as The One That Got Away.

When she got down to the street, he was leaning against the driver's side door of his car. As she appeared, he smiled, coming to his feet as he walked around to the passenger's side of the car, intercepting her there as he opened the door for her. Before she could slip past him right into the car, he touched her forearm with his fingers, her eyes finding his warm and open, with nothing held back.

"Hi," was all he said, the pressure from his fingertips inviting her to lean forward, to accept an embrace, a kiss on the cheek, some display of affection that right now felt entirely too much to bear.

"Hi," was all she said back, forcing a smile and breaking eye contact as she snuck past him and into the car. This would all be easier if she didn't have to feel his arms around her, smell his comforting smell, be so immersed in *him*.

Not that sitting mere inches away from him in his car was exactly the solution she would have hoped for. A solid steel door between them would be more effective, or perhaps the width of the Bosphorus would be enough to do the trick.

As Burak entered on the other side of the car, sliding into his own seat, he shot a glance at her. "Everything okay?" he asked, and she noted the concern in his voice.

"Mm hmm." She nodded, but she still didn't look at him. "It seemed like the cats settled into their new home really well. I did a head count when I left this evening, and there wasn't even one kitten out of place."

Burak exhaled out of his nose in an approximation of a laugh. "I'm glad to hear it. What about you, though? That's what I meant, actually. You seemed...I don't know. On edge about something? Is everything okay with you?"

Jasmine really didn't want to have this conversation *now*. Not when he was behind the wheel, and not when there was an entire evening ahead of the two of them that was supposed to be full of good food and good company.

"Just tired," she said at last. "It's nice to be going out and celebrating, even if there's a part of me that would have been just fine curling up on the couch in my sweats and zoning out in front of a movie."

Burak glanced away from the road then, his eyes serious when they found hers. "If that's what you want, that's okay with me." His cheeks flushed as he focused back on the traffic ahead of them. "I mean, I'd be happy to join you, but I'm also happy to reschedule if you prefer to be alone."

There was a twinge in her chest at his sincerity, at the vulnerability with which he had invited himself along, and then retracted his words as if they were spoken in error. She could imagine slipping so effortlessly into a comfortable routine with Burak, too many nights curled up on the couch to count until they finally forced themselves to venture out into the "real world," to trade takeout in for the view of a beautiful sunset. Maybe in another life...

"This will be fun," she said. And then, because she couldn't resist at least dropping a hint that would keep his hopes from rising to a point too high he might be crushed in the fall: "I should go out and enjoy Istanbul every chance I have, after all, since I don't know how much longer I'll be around."

Burak's lips pulled to the side, a twinge that looked as if he had tasted something sour, but he didn't speak.

The conversation wasn't supposed to flow, and the evening wasn't supposed to feel like the beginning of something. It was *supposed* to be a nice break from routine, a chance for whatever connection had bloomed between Jasmine and Burak to be acknowledged, appreciated, and laid to rest.

But things didn't always go the way they were supposed to, and there was no truth that Jasmine was surer of than that.

From the moment Burak had parked the car and come around to open her door for her, she had known she was in trouble. He had selected, judging by where he was leaving the car at least, to show her the best that Istanbul had to offer. They were close enough to the water that she could hear the seagulls, a thrill of anticipation rushing through her as they began to walk.

The early evening sun was reflecting off the water, colors painted across the sky that made Jasmine think of Taylor Swift's "Lover" album cover, adding further fuel to her suspicion that she was in trouble.

"I thought we could walk a bit, take in the sights. Is that alright with you?" Burak asked, glancing down at her feet. "If you didn't wear walking shoes, we can find a closer restaurant, or drive some more."

She looked down at her shoes with him, grateful for the opportunity not to make eye contact. It was little considerations like this that continued to set him apart. "I'll be fine. I've always wanted to explore Istanbul more than I have, but I just got so busy with the cafe." She looked around then. "Where are we, anyway? What is this neighborhood?"

"Ah, yes. I've brought you to the most touristy part of Istanbul, the sights you see on all the postcards. But it's not like Times Square, I promise. People actually live here, and Turkish people actually come here, too." He gestured around them then. "This, my dear, is Sultanahmet. We will take a short walk around and in no time at all you'll see the Blue Mosque, the Hagia Sophia, and plenty of other beautiful and old buildings that you won't even be able to remember them all. How does that sound?"

"Amazing," she said in all sincerity. It was the precise evening she had dreamed of spending in Istanbul, the sort she had to explain *not* having to her travel-savvy friends who popped up on Instagram from time to time, asking her what she thought of the city and then relaying their own "24 hours in Istanbul" experiences and all the sights they had seen.

It was the perfect way to say goodbye.

Jasmine smiled at Burak and fell into step beside him, her own personal tour guide to one of the most beautiful cities she had ever seen. His interest in architecture served her well, too, as he filled her in on intricacies of the buildings and the architects who had dreamed them into existence that she was sure her friends hadn't learned on their whirlwind tours.

Finally, after she had snapped her thousandth photo, as jaw dropping as the first, they were standing on the edge of the Bosphorus, the sun now fully set as the lights from the nearby buildings reflected off the water.

Burak turned to face her, a sincerity in his eyes that sounded the warning bell in Jasmine's lizard brain. *Danger*, it was warning her. *This man is about to get serious. He's going to say things you can't unhear, and you need to put a stop to it before it happens.*

"Should we go get something to eat now?" she blurted, her hand coming to her stomach in the sort of gesture a hungry person would make, or at least an approximation of it. Her appetite had vanished, either due to her heightened level of excitement at exploring Istanbul or in anticipation of the conversation she needed to have with Burak.

"Absolutely," he said. "Would you prefer something we can grab to go and eat here or sitting down in a restaurant?"

"Grab and go," she blurted. The less romantic the setting, the better. An image of sitting across a candlelit table from Burak, holding a glass of wine by its stem as his eyes bored into hers flashed in her mind's eye.

If Burak had noticed her abrupt nature, had picked up on the anxiety that was causing it, he didn't say anything. He led her to a nearby döner stand, where they ordered two kebabs and ayran before making their way back to an empty bench near the water.

A few bites into her sandwich, Jasmine plucked up the courage to do what needed to be done. "I like you," she said, the words tumbling out quickly enough to surprise both of them.

"I—" Burak began, but Jasmine held up a hand to stop him from speaking further, from saying something she couldn't unhear. For once, she wasn't afraid a crush of hers was about to reveal that he thought she was a swamp troll, but the opposite. She knew his feelings already, and it would only make her impending departure that much more difficult.

"I like you, *but*—"

"I knew there would be a but." It was Burak's turn to interrupt her, and his eyes were downcast as he shook his head.

"The but isn't about you," she hurried to explain. "But it's a big but. I mean…I'm going to leave soon. My grandmother will come back and move back into her apartment and start running the cafe again, and there just won't be any point in me being here."

The expression on Burak's face was unreadable, but it was curious, no longer downcast. "Did she tell you that?"

Jasmine shook her head. "No. We're supposed to talk tonight, actually. After I get back home…or, to her apartment, I mean. Not my home. And you know as well as I do that she's not a cold person, not unkind at all. She would never kick me out of her apartment, would never tell me that it was time for me to get on with my life." She sighed then. "But she has a beautiful life, Burak. A lovely home, a job to keep her busy that I know fills her heart with so many warm fuzzies, a relationship that supports her…and she should have the space to enjoy all of those things without me stepping on her toes and taking up her space."

"She might argue that having you there in her space would only make all of those things better."

Jasmine nodded. "You're right. But it just doesn't sit right with me. It's one thing to be here when I'm helping her out, but it's something entirely different to stay on once she's back and perfectly capable of doing everything herself. It changes me from the one providing help to the one *being* helped, and I'm not sure I'm comfortable with that."

Burak cocked his head at an angle as his eyes finally met hers. "That might be worth examining, Jas. If you're comfortable giving help but not receiving it…it's just interesting, is all. It might suggest that you think one of those positions is the superior one to be in, and in that case, helping someone else out might not be as selfless as you think it is. It might be nothing more than an ego trip dressed up as a good deed."

Her mouth dropped at his words. "I...what? How dare you, Burak? I mean..." She shook her head. The last thing she needed was a sick burn like that, to be kicked while she was already down.

Though it was possible he was also doing her a favor on some level...his words *did* make it easier to want to say goodbye to him tonight and not regret what could have been.

Just as she was about to get to her feet and storm off in the direction of a taxi, she felt the weight of Burak's hand on her forearm.

"I'm sorry," he said. "That was uncalled for and probably not what you needed to hear in the moment. I wasn't trying to accuse you of anything, but just trying to be helpful, if you can believe it." He chuckled then, just once. "That was a lesson I learned myself, actually, not that long ago, thanks to your grandmother. I used to always want to be on the giving end of the things, picking up your grandmother's morning pastry for her and shooting her down when she tried to buy mine for me. I realized it might have been at least partially borne out of an unwillingness to ask for help. And if I hadn't listened to your grandmother, hadn't accepted her help and been willing to ask for yours and for Enes's..." He trailed off, his eyes on the water. "Well, you and I probably wouldn't be here."

The smile he gave her then was small, but it wasn't sad, not defeated in the way that Jasmine would have expected. It was almost as if he was unwilling to accept what she had told him, as if he couldn't yet believe that she was going to leave, that there was no future between them.

She was quiet then, unsure of what else to say. He knew what her plans were, at least as far as leaving went. Neither one of them knew what would come after that.

"We can keep hanging out until I leave," she offered, her voice small enough to surprise her. "I just didn't want you to think there was any real future here. But can we be friends?"

His gaze was intent. "Of course we can. And I want to talk to you tomorrow, after you've spoken with your grandmother." He glanced at his watch then. "I should get you home. It's important for the two of you to connect."

Though Jasmine was surprised at how disappointed she felt at the impending end of the evening, she knew it wasn't exactly fair to object. It wasn't as if she had told Burak something he would be particularly jazzed to hear, and if he wanted to part ways to lick his wounds, then who was she to insist they stay out for just one more drink?

They walked back to his car, the silence between them tinged with something that hadn't been there before. Even just a few hours before, any lapses in conversation had been comfortable—and short, quick to be filled with a joke, a story, a tidbit of Istanbul history that had equal odds of being made up, an elaborate joke, or a genuinely fascinating fact.

The change in the tone of the empty air between them flooded Jasmine with an unwelcome sadness. Not only was it completely inconvenient and impractical for her to want to keep Burak in her life, but she had been just fine without him only a few weeks prior. Surely she wouldn't perish from a Burak deficiency when she left Istanbul, and there was no reason not to start reducing her exposure to him in the meantime.

"Thanks for a nice evening," she said when he pulled to a stop in front of her apartment. She put a hand up to stop him as he reached for his seatbelt. "It's okay, you don't need to walk me in. I can wave down from the living room if you want to be sure I made it inside safely."

She had been mostly joking, but his nod suggested that he was taking her completely seriously. "I would prefer to walk you up myself, but I'll settle for a wave. Otherwise my mind is going to keep me up all night wondering if there was a hitman waiting for you inside or something equally chilling."

She turned her head to the side, looking at him from the side. "If you think that's a likely option, you probably watch too many thrillers. Just to be safe, though, should we have a secret signal? Some way for me to wave down at you and make it look to the hitman like everything is okay, while I'm also alerting you to his presence?"

"That's a great idea," Burak deadpanned. "And it can't be something obvious like a thumbs up, thumbs down situation, because he'd definitely see right through that. What about waving with your left hand if everything is safe and fine and with your right hand if it isn't?"

Jasmine shook her head. "I've already forgotten which is which, and I can't risk you breaking down my grandmother's door just because we forgot to decide if it was *my* right or your right, you know?" She paused then, with her hand on the door handle. "What if it's the position of my non-waving hand? I could put it over my heart if everything is okay, or I could touch the back of my neck if it isn't?"

Burak nodded, leaning forward then to kiss her on the cheek. "Perfect. I'll be waiting."

As she closed the car door behind her, there was a pang of knowing. It was very likely the last time she would be climbing out of Burak's car, waving at him through the window, unable to stop herself from smiling back at him, at the genuine joy he seemed to feel when his eyes were on hers.

You're being absurd, she chided herself. *Again.* She hurried up the stairs and into her apartment, barely greeting the cats before making a beeline to the window. When she looked down, there he was, looking up at her expectantly. Jasmine smiled at him, waving, as she placed her hand on her heart. Burak smiled back, waving once more before putting his car in gear and driving away.

Jasmine flopped onto the couch with a loud sigh. Cheddar and Gator were quick to join her there, and she scratched them both behind the ears, letting the sound of purring ground her back into the present moment.

As if on cue, her phone began to ring with an incoming video call from her grandmother. Jasmine forced the unwelcome thoughts from her mind and smiled as she answered the call, surprised by the flood of emotion she felt at the sight of her grandmother's face.

"Grandma!" she cried, swallowing the lump that had risen in her throat. "Oh my God, I miss you so much. I knew I missed you, but I didn't know how much until just now."

Viola Brody smiled back at her granddaughter, and she was the very picture of retired bliss and joy. She was glowing, as cliche as it sounded, and Jasmine couldn't believe how well she was suited for life on a boat. While Jasmine would probably be green from sea sickness, her grandmother looked like she had replaced stress with sun, SPF, and good living.

"Hi dear! I missed you, too. Is that Gator on your lap? Lift the camera up, love, I don't want to see his butt."

Jasmine laughed despite the emotion she was feeling, lifting the phone with one hand and using her other hand to direct Gator's jaw so that Viola could see her cat's face.

"He misses you too," she said, "And I'm sure he's very happy you'll be back soon."

"Ah yes," said Viola, with just a hint of hesitation in her voice. Jasmine turned the phone again so that only her face was on the screen, Gator hopping off the couch in search of food, and she raised an eyebrow at her grandmother. "That's what I wanted to talk to you about," said Viola.

"Okay..."

"Are...are you liking it in Istanbul? Would you be up for staying longer? I don't want you to do anything you aren't comfortable with..."

"Oh, it's been great," Jasmine rushed to explain. "But I don't want to be in your hair. I'll move on when you come back." She forced a brightness into her words that she didn't feel. "I'm not sure yet where I'll go, but that's part of the fun of it all, isn't it?"

There was a hint of deflation in her grandmother's face. "That's wonderful," she said. "I just want you to be happy. I'll figure out a different plan. Don't you worry about it at all."

Jasmine frowned. That wasn't what she had expected to hear at all. "What do you mean, Grandma? A different plan for what? Aren't you coming back?"

"I'm coming back, but just to get things in order. Morty and I want to...well, we want to make this whole 'cruising the world' thing a lifestyle. Keep going for as long as we can. I didn't realize it was the sort of thing that people made a life out of until we got here and started making connections. And well, I think I figured out what I want to do when I grow up...or at least when I retire, which, technically, I am. But it's fine, dear, if you don't want to stay on in Istanbul. I don't want to chain you down with the cafe, and I'm sure I could find someone else to do it or even sell it or—"

"I'll do it," Jasmine interrupted. Her voice wobbled and as she looked down at her hands, she saw they were shaking. Was this really happening?

Viola's face spread with a broad smile. "Really? I mean...do you *really* want to do that? I don't want you to take it on just because you feel obligated. There's a whole big world out there for you to explore, and you're going to get sick of making coffee if you never get to see any of it."

Jasmine shook her head. "It's exactly what I want. And trust me, I have you exploring more than enough for the both of us. Will you send me postcards from the cruise stops? I want to decorate a whole wall with them. Maybe link them with yarn to trace your route and make the whole thing look like it's a mad detective's attempt at solving a crime. And I'm sure I'll take a vacation here and there, too. Plus, it's not like I've even explored a tiny fraction of all Istanbul has to offer." She had to stop herself from clapping her hands and squealing. "Is this real life, Grandma? Are we really doing this?"

"We are, dear." Viola nodded. "And I can't tell you how happy it makes me."

Sixteen

The first thing Jasmine wanted to do when the call ended was tell Burak, of course. But when the thought popped into her mind that maybe he was only telling her he wanted her to stay when in reality he was relieved to have a "get out of jail free" card as far as their relationship was concerned, she put down the phone, leaving it in the living room to charge while she went into the spare bedroom and dug out her paints and an abandoned canvas.

"Sorry boys," she told Cheddar and Gator as she closed the door between them. "Cats and wet paint don't go together."

Jasmine lost herself on the canvas for the first time in ages. Maybe it was the news that she was putting down roots, that she was *home* for good now, that there was no big "next step" weighing on her that demanded to be figured out in the near future. The colors whirled, her brush moving freely as she focused only on how it felt to see the canvas transform, with no concern for what the end result might be.

For once, it wasn't about creating something specific, about a product that would have commercial value or be appreciated by anyone else who looked at it. The only thing that mattered was this moment, the joy of playing with color and texture, the feel of the brush gliding across the surface, and the glorious and entirely unfamiliar way her mind emptied itself of worries and concerns.

If it wasn't a metaphor for life, she didn't know what was.

By the time Jasmine had washed the paint from her hands and fallen into bed, the lightness had permeated all the way to her bones. She hadn't known how heavily the impending stresses had been weighing on her until they were gone. But now, her concerns about what would happen to the cats, what could have been with Burak, and where she would be resting her head...all of it was gone, replaced with gratitude. No matter what happened with Burak, even if his face fell when she told him the news and he made a graceful exit from her life, she was home and the future was bright.

Seventeen

J asmine's first stop in the morning, before she even unlocked the door of the cafe, was the courtyard. A tiny tuxedo kitten ran over to greet her, twining around her legs and filling her heart close to bursting. The cats looked even more at home than they had in the old lot, and she was once again in awe of how quickly things could change. How quickly a strange place could come to feel like home.

She crouched down to greet the kitten when she heard a throat clear behind her. Before she even turned to face the sound, she knew it was Burak and her heart picked up at just the nearness of him.

"Hi," she squeaked, the size of her smile and the volume of her voice inversely proportional.

His mouth pulled up at one corner. "What are you so happy about?" he asked, then shook his head. "By which I mean, of course, good morning. It's lovely to see you."

"It's lovely to see you, too," she replied. "And I have some news to share with you."

"Good news, I hope?"

Jasmine nodded. "I think so, and I hope you will, too."

"Well, don't tease me, please. What is it?"

She smiled. "You don't want to wait until we're inside with cups of coffee in front of us?"

Burak shook his head. "No, I don't think I can. I have...let's say, a *suspicion* of what it might be, and I can't wait to find out if I'm correct."

"Interesting." She stood up and took a tentative step towards him. "Well, I spoke with my grandmother last night."

"Right." He took another step towards her. "And what did Ms. Viola say?"

"Oh, you know..." Jasmine paused for a second, unable to stop herself from smiling, while knowing her cheeks were heating at the same time. "She wants to keep living the glamorous cruise lifestyle. And she wants me to stay on here, running the cafe."

Burak's face split into a broad grin as he rushed towards her and pulled her into his arms. At the last second, he reared back to look at her face. "Did you say yes? Before I congratulate you and tell you how happy I am, please confirm for me that you said yes."

Jasmine barely had time to nod before Burak was embracing her, lifting her off her feet, and twirling her around. She threw her head back, letting her gleeful laughter flow. When he finally set her back down, she saw her expression mirrored in his own.

"So we can keep being friends," she offered, swallowing. "If you still want that, I mean."

"I still want that. Or perhaps I should remind you that I want more than that." He lifted her hand to his lips, placing a warm kiss across the back of her knuckles. "Can I cook for you tonight? Have a do-over of our date now that we both know this thing between us is going somewhere?"

She raised an eyebrow. "Oh, it's going somewhere, is it?" She smiled at him then, unabashed by the vulnerability she saw in his eyes, the way he made no attempt to hide or downplay his interest in her. "Then it's a date."

Author's Note

This series has been a lot of fun to write, incorporating my favorite feline quirks in every new installment. Book 3 of the Cats of Istanbul novella series, *Whiskers and Wanderlust*, is coming in 2024.

To stay updated on other works in progress or purchase books and bundles directly from me, please visit my website at kcmccormickciftci.com.

If you loved this book, please consider leaving a review, as that is one of the best ways to support indie authors like me. Reviews left on major retail sites (wherever you bought this book is a great start!), review sites, and Book-Bub will help other readers discover this book, too.

About the Author

KC McCormick Çiftçi is an English teacher turned romance writer. She spent the majority of her twenties living and working abroad, collecting the experiences that inform the stories she tells. She enjoys telling multicultural and international love stories through romantic comedy and women's fiction. She lives in Turkey with her husband and a herd of cats.

Prior to diving into the world of romance, KC published two self-help books for intercultural couples, *Loving Across Borders* and *The K-1 Visa Wedding Plan*. Both are available wherever books are sold.

For updates on upcoming releases, behind the scenes news, and all my favorite book recommendations, visit kcmccormickciftci.com (or just point your phone camera at the QR code below).

Books by KC McCormick Çiftçi

Austen in Turkey

Pride, Prejudice, & Turkish Delight

Sense, Sensibility, & the Mediterranean Sea

Home (Abroad) for the Holidays

Christmas on Inishmore

Christmas at Terminal One

Intoxicated by You

Intoxicated by You

Cats of Istanbul

The Vet Upstairs

From Strays to Soulmates

Intercultural Relationship Self Help

Loving Across Borders

The K-1 Visa Wedding Plan